D1572705

PREGNANCY

*Private
Decisions,*
Public
Debates

KATHLYN GAY

Women Then—Women Now
Franklin Watts
New York Chicago London Toronto Sydney

Library of Congress Cataloging-in-Publication Data

Gay, Kathlyn.
    Pregnancy : private decisions, public debates, c1993.
        p.   cm.—(Women then—women now)
    Includes bibliographical references and index.
    ISBN 0-531-11167-9
    1. Birth Control—United States—Moral and ethical aspects.
    2. Conception—Moral and ethical aspects.   3. Contraception—United
    States—Moral and ethical aspects.   4. Human reproductive
    technology—United States.   I. Title.   II. Series.
    HQ766.15.G39   1993
    363.9'6'0973—dc20   93-29456 CIP AC

CONTENTS

CONFLICTS OVER
REPRODUCTIVE
DECISIONS

Bree Walker, an anchorwoman for a Los Angeles television station, and her husband, Jim Lampley, a network sportscaster, decided to have a baby. Usually such a decision is a private matter, but it became a subject for public debate in 1991 when Jane Norris, a local radio talk show hostess, invited comments about Walker's pregnancy. Norris informed her listening audience that Walker had a 50 percent chance of bearing a child who would inherit a genetic condition known as ectrodactylism, in which the bones of fingers or toes fuse and form webbed hands or feet. Walker has the condition, as does her daughter from a previous marriage. Norris disapproved of Walker's childbearing decision, as did numerous listeners who called in to air their views. But others called to support Walker and her husband. The couple's daughter, who was born in the fall of 1991, inherited the genetic condition, and from all accounts, she and family are doing fine.[1]

A pregnant North Dakota woman, Martina Greywind, became the center of a public controversy in 1992 after she was arrested for drug abuse and endangering her fetus. Greywind wanted an abortion, and conflict erupted when an aggressive anti-abortion group called the Lambs of Christ tried to pressure Greywind to carry her fetus to term, offering to pay her

$11,000. Her brother spoke out against the offer, saying his sister was being exploited and was incapable of caring for a child, since she had practically abandoned six other children. Greywind had been addicted to drugs for years and had been arrested numerous times for intoxication due to inhaling paint vapors. Because of this, family members and friends cared for her offspring. Greywind has also been committed to a mental hospital for short periods, but after each release she has lived on the streets. Just twelve days after Greywind's story was publicized, she had an abortion. Charges against her were dropped. Although her family and many social workers have attempted to get treatment for Greywind, they believe she now suffers from brain damage and they have little hope that she will improve.[2]

A former East Coast couple, Steven and Risa York, who were unable to have children, became embroiled in a legal battle after they participated in a Virginia medical program during the 1980s in which they were able to use Risa's eggs and Steven's sperm to artificially create embryos, organisms in the early stage of development. The embryos were preserved by freezing them in a tank of liquid nitrogen. Risa attempted eleven times to have an embryo implanted in her womb with the hope that a pregnancy would result, but she was unsuccessful. When the Yorks moved to California, they wanted to have a twelfth frozen embryo transferred to a Los Angeles clinic near their home, so that Risa could try another implant. But the Virginia clinic refused to allow the transfer because of the possibility that the embryo might be destroyed en route. The Yorks sued the Virginia clinic, and in 1989 a judge ordered the release of the embryo to the Yorks.[3]

At first glance, these three situations seem unrelated, but they share common ground. They represent only some of the varied reproductive issues that have been widely discussed and debated over the past thirty years. They are also examples of the increasing number of instances in which the public—

through the media, government, or activist groups—has intervened in private reproductive decisions.

Since human reproduction can have long-term effects on a society, childbearing can create public concern. For example, some pregnant women who do not receive appropriate prenatal care may damage their own health and perhaps deliver a baby with severe physical or mental disabilities. If parents do not have the resources to rear a child with severe handicaps, public and private agencies may have to provide needed services. Thus medical, religious, and governmental officials and citizen groups within a society may encourage or try to force a pregnant women to obtain proper health care or to follow established patterns of behavior to protect her health.

No matter how well intended such interventions may be, they can lead to conflicts. Getting pregnant, carrying a fetus, and delivering a baby are intensely personal matters, and increasingly, women are demanding the freedom to make their own choices. Women want to make informed decisions about their reproductive functions and health practices before and during pregnancy and childbirth.

SOME ISSUES UNDER FIRE

Since the 1960s and 1970s, the right to reproductive choice has usually been interpreted to mean the right to abort, or terminate, a pregnancy. Certainly abortion is a major issue, but it is not the only one to create controversy.

Some conflicts have developed because of new reproductive technologies (NRTs). Some of these new technologies have helped women who have been unable to become pregnant to have children. They have also made surrogate motherhood possible. In a surrogate arrangement, a woman agrees to be a substitute carrier for the fetus, producing and delivering a child for those who contract for her services. Critics denounce the practice, arguing that women are being used and, in effect, are renting out their wombs to grow a fetus. Usually, when a surrogate mother gives birth, she must also give up any "natural" rights to the child she bore. So questions are raised about whose rights are paramount.

NRTs may also create conflicts when a pregnant woman is pressured to accept fetal therapy, surgical procedures on the fetus recommended by medical practitioners. Women who are opposed to surgery or question the safety of fetal therapy procedures believe they should have the right to refuse such treatment. But some people condemn women who refuse fetal therapy, insisting that the women are endangering a potential life.

The treatment of pregnant women who are drug abusers is another major issue. Some people argue that drug addicts who give birth to addicted children should be prosecuted, jailed, and required to use birth control. Others say there should be more treatment facilities and health programs for women who abuse drugs, to protect the lives of both the mothers and their children. Another closely related issue raises the question of whether the government should force the sterilization of some women as punishment for their illegal behavior or to prevent the birth of children with disabilities.

Interventions in the lives of pregnant teenagers and the kinds of jobs pregnant women are allowed to perform in the workplace are two other issues being debated. Another is the lack of adequate prenatal health care for a great number of poor women, which may result in severely underweight, handicapped, and drug-addicted infants.

Other reproductive controversies develop over differences in the way people view fundamental, or natural, rights, which include the right to be free of government intervention and coercion. Natural rights are based on the concept of individual liberty—the belief that a person should have the freedom to make her or his own decisions and to act upon them, as long as those actions do not violate the rights of others. But whether or not certain reproductive decisions and actions infringe upon others' rights is often difficult to determine.

Religious views and beliefs about who should control reproductive matters can also spark debates. Cultural patterns

—the way of life of certain groups of people—may determine who makes decisions in regard to procreation and whose rights are paramount.

Finally, population control is a reproductive issue of worldwide significance. Some population experts are convinced that population control is essential in order to prevent global economic and social disaster. They predict that in the near future there will be a short supply of basic resources available to sustain a world population growing by 90 million people a year. Others argue that overpopulation is not the problem. Instead, they feel that the major difficulty is distributing needed resources on a more equitable basis.

Resolutions to many, if not most, reproductive issues may be impossible. But the questions raised may prompt further inquiry and thoughtful discussions, a first step toward resolving social concerns.

*Chapter
Two*

CHILDBEARING
AND THE SOCIAL
STRUCTURE

Individual attitudes, beliefs, and opinions about childbearing vary greatly, but a person's views on reproduction are not necessarily her or his own. Views about procreation may be shaped by one's family, cultural group, and the larger society. In other words, social customs, laws, and religious beliefs influence many decisions about human reproduction and the reasons people have children. As Ruth Hubbard, a biology professor at Harvard, explained, "Just as our sexual practices are socially constructed and not a natural unfolding of inborn instincts, so our ways of structuring and experiencing pregnancy and birth are shaped by society."[1]

WHY PEOPLE HAVE CHILDREN

Certainly one of the basic reasons people have children is biological: the sex instinct, or drive, helps assure that the human species will continue to reproduce. But social and economic motivations may be even more significant in decisions to have children.

In the past, when most Americans depended on agriculture for a living and produced most of their own furniture and clothing, families usually included many children because they were needed to help with the labor. Parents also wanted offspring so that when they grew old there would be children to care for them. Some families today still depend on children to work in the fields, hunt, fish, take care of domestic animals, and provide care for younger siblings and eventually the family's elderly.

Another reason people have children is because of cultural patterns. Some cultural groups in a society believe that as their numbers increase so does their power. According to this reasoning, a group with many members will have more opportunities to gain political influence or will be able to spread the group's religious beliefs. Members of such groups encourage large families, assuming that children will be taught to support a particular political view or a group's religious faith.

People are also motivated for various personal reasons to have children. Some want to prove that they can reproduce or make sure that the family name will continue. Couples may have children because they do not feel they are a family if they are childless, although that view has changed drastically over the past few decades. Family structures today are varied; they include couples who choose to be childless, parents and children who are not biologically related (as in stepfamilies), and single parents with children.

FROM MAGNA MATER TO THE DOMINANT FATHER

Social customs and cultural patterns that help to determine childbearing decisions continually change. But *control* of the social structure, wherever it exists, has remained fairly constant for thousands of years. Worldwide, social systems—whether economic, educational, medical, legal, political, scientific, or religious—have been dominated by men. Thus male views and decisions determine how societies will function. Men frequently define women's roles and enforce the accepted conduct for women, including how pregnant women or potentially pregnant women should behave.

Yet men have not always controlled women and their

reproductive choices. Tens of thousands of years ago, people believed that women were endowed with supernatural, life-giving powers. Because women brought forth life, female spirits were credited with controlling all the mysterious workings of life and death, including the ability to change day into night. People worshipped female deities, goddesses who reigned over food production and human reproduction.

Many scholars have brushed aside the idea of a female deity, but statues and temples unearthed in many parts of the world indicate that belief in a divine goddess was widespread. A Great-Mother Goddess was worshipped in many parts of the ancient world. She was known by such names as Magna Mater (Rome), Isis (Egypt), and Ishtar (Babylonia).

Woman were also priests and held other positions of honor in prehistoric times. In fact, women dominated some early societies. Archaeological evidence shows that such societies were matriarchies—children were given their mother's name and daughters inherited their mother's property. Sons could not inherit. Fathers turned over whatever they earned or captured to the woman's clan.[2]

However, when people learned that males contributed to the reproduction of the human species, women's dominant position began to change. The development of agriculture also contributed to the decline of women's status. Women were on a par with men when tribes moved from place to place, because women gathered the food and carried the burdens, leaving men free to hunt. But as nomadic groups began to settle in one place, grow much of their food, and accumulate property, including serfs or slaves, women began to lose their value as workers.

For a time, clan groups owned property collectively, but eventually individual families took the place of clans and amassed property and wealth. Men took over property rights and formed patriarchal societies, which meant that property was inherited by sons or the eldest males in the family. Women were considered property, as were the children they were expected to bear, particularly male children who would inherit the wealth controlled by the father.

Over the centuries, religious views and practices contributed to the suppression of women. While some ancient cultures continued to worship multiple gods and goddesses, people in Judea (now a part of Israel), who became known as Jews, believed in a single male god. Religious laws dominated the society, and Jewish patriarchs interpreted and enforced the laws.

The belief in a single male god and the concept of male dominance carried over to Christianity and eventually to almost all parts of the social structure in the western world. Male scholars developed theories contending that women were born to be subservient caregivers (just as others tried to prove that certain groups were born to be slaves).

Based on such theories, women were thought to be suitable only for procreation, rearing children, and caring for men —unless the women were needed to engage in war, work on the farms, or provide other labor for the benefit of society. Yet no evidence has proven that nurturing is an inborn female trait or that women have a lock on such attributes as compassion, kindness, and mercy. Men also exhibit these characteristics.

Over the past few decades, some sociologists and other researchers have concluded that people are socialized to behave in gender-specific ways. In other words, people tend to assume roles determined by the culture into which they are born. Children identify with their parents and learn gender roles from them. Toys children play with, the language they learn, and the images they see of their gender in the mass media reinforce what is considered appropriate feminine or masculine behavior.

Gender stereotyping has helped justify social customs and laws that have denied women educations, jobs, ownership of property, voting rights, and countless other privileges that men have enjoyed over the ages. Nevertheless, throughout history some women have refused to be defined by their biology or their social conditioning.

THE SEARCH FOR EQUITY

Until about the 1860s, American women had few civil rights. Married women, for example, could not own property—not even their clothing. All material goods legally belonged to the husband, as did the children of a marriage. If a married woman worked, she could be forced to turn over her wages to her husband and could not divorce unless her husband consented.

When women began to organize and demand the freedom to make reproductive choices, they faced a "firestorm of opposition," as Pulitzer Prize-winning journalist Susan Faludi describes it in her book *Backlash: The Undeclared War Against Women.* "All of women's aspirations—whether for education, work, or any form of self-determination—ultimately rest on their ability to decide whether and when to bear children. For this reason, reproductive freedom has always been the most popular item" in the women's rights movement and a target for backlash, Faludi states.[3]

Today, as in the past, women who demand reproductive choices still face much opposition, principally from individuals and groups who object to women's independence and their attempts to attain equal status with men. Opponents believe women should be part of what has been called the "typical" or "traditional" family—a family structure established as an ideal around the 1930s. At that time, an increasing number of Americans of white European ancestry had become part of the middle class, and women were encouraged to stay in the home, perform household tasks, and produce and care for children while men earned income outside the home.

During World War II, factories and businesses eagerly sought women for jobs vacated by men in the armed forces. But after the fighting ended, women returned to domestic chores and child care, leaving their jobs to male workers. Some people believe that this idealized family structure—father as wage earner and mother as caregiver—should dominate today, arguing that it is the only way to preserve "family values," which in many cases means emphasizing patriarchial views and making women and children subservient to men. But that family structure is no longer common in the United States (and never was for poor families who could not have survived without the income that women earned).

At present, the so-called traditional family is in the minority. The most common family unit is a married couple with no children, but that family structure includes young couples who plan to have children and older couples whose children have left home. According to a 1993 U.S. Census report, 25.5 percent of all United States households in 1992 consisted of married couples with children under age eighteen.[4] But many children will spend a part of their childhood in a single-parent home.

A majority of families today include mothers who are employed outside the home, so many women are pressuring for equity in their households, with men sharing in parenting and household tasks. In addition, women who literally carry the burden of childbearing are attempting to exercise what they consider to be their natural rights in matters of reproduction. Many women want to make choices about reproduction that will meet their specific needs and those of the people with whom they share their lives.

Chapter
Three

BIRTH CONTROL—A
CONTROVERSIAL
ISSUE

In order to schedule childbearing to meet their own needs, some women and their partners choose to prevent pregnancy at various times in their lives. Others choose to remain childless. But in many cases, pregnancy prevention can be difficult. Many Americans, unlike the majority of Europeans, do not have easy access to information on contraception, the means of preventing pregnancy.

Most European countries have conducted extensive research on pregnancy prevention and have developed educational programs on birth control. In the United States, research to develop new contraceptives has been cut back; only one new birth control method, Norplant, has been introduced in recent years.

Contraception has long been a controversial issue in the United States and has sometimes caused heated arguments. On one side are people who believe that families should be able to plan and control the number and spacing of their children or to decide whether they want to have children at all. They believe birth control devices and family planning programs should be available on a broad basis across the United States and worldwide.

On the other side are individuals who believe that any family planning methods that include mechanical devices—contraceptives—are morally wrong. They say that couples should engage in sexual intercourse for one primary purpose: to create life. They believe that birth control devices prevent a man and woman from being together spiritually as one, and that contraceptives encourage people to use sex primarily for pleasure.

WHAT IS BIRTH CONTROL?

For those who oppose any mechanical means of contraception, the acceptable forms of birth control include complete abstinence (no sexual contact) and the so-called natural or rhythm method, which depends on a woman's cycle of ovulation. If a couple uses such a method, they must know when the woman ovulates, or when a ripe egg moves from a woman's ovary into her fallopian tube where it can be fertilized by the man's sperm. If a couple avoids sexual intercourse during ovulation, a period of one to several days, pregnancy may be prevented. But the trick is to know exactly when ovulation takes place and to time intercourse so that it occurs only when a woman is infertile. The method may work very well for some people, but frequently is unreliable.

People who have no objections to mechanical means of preventing conception use either chemical or barrier devices. There is not space to describe in detail the varied contraceptive devices available, but here is just a brief look at some contraceptives that health officials might suggest.

Chemical contraceptives include creams, jellies, or foams that contain spermicides—substances that kill sperm cells—and are inserted into the vagina before intercourse. Barrier devices include the diaphragm that covers the female cervix and opening to the uterus, and the condom, a stretchable latex sheath that covers the male penis.

One of the most popular and effective means of birth control is ingesting a synthetic female hormone in pill form. Known as "the Pill," the medication suppresses ovulation so conception cannot take place. The medication is taken for three or four weeks each month.

A new contraceptive known as Norplant uses the same synthetic hormone as the Pill, except that the hormone is in silicone capsules, each the size of a matchstick. In a painless procedure that takes ten or fifteen minutes, a doctor implants the flexible tubes, arranging them like a fan, in a woman's inner arm above the elbow where they can be felt but not seen. Low doses of the hormone are released steadily into the bloodstream, inhibiting ovulation and making it difficult for sperm to reach the egg. The implants can provide protection for up to five years.

Norplant has been marketed and used successfully in dozens of countries since 1983. But it was not available in the United States until 1991, after extensive testing by the U.S. Food and Drug Administration (FDA). The device is expected to be even more effective, less expensive in the long run, and safer than the Pill, the FDA reported.[1]

Sterilization is the leading method of contraception among married couples in the United States, according to the Institute of Medicine. For both men and women, sterilization involves surgery. A vasectomy is performed on men; a section of each of the sperm tubes is removed and the tubes tied. Tubal ligation for women is similar except that the fallopian tubes are cut or cauterized and tied. In some cases, women have hysterectomies —the uterus is surgically removed to prevent pregnancy— although this procedure is not recommended for contraceptive purposes only.

Other types of birth control methods may become available in the United States in the future, such as a vaccine that stimulates a woman's immune system to produce antibodies that prevent the male sperm from fertilizing an egg and a contraceptive pill called RU-486. The vaccine is already under development by Ortho Pharmaceutical. But RU-486, which has been used successfully in France (where it was developed) and several other European nations, was banned for personal use in the United States until 1993, when President Bill Clinton revoked the prohibition pending the FDA's approval of safety.

Although the drug could be an effective contraceptive, it is primarily an abortifacient—a chemical that causes abortion. Thus United States anti-abortion groups campaigned to prevent import of the drug for clinical testing and use. (The debate over this so-called abortion pill is described in the next chapter.)

Although new contraceptives would be developed primarily for women, there is the possibility that a male birth control pill will be available by the year 2000. The male pill will make use of a synthetic male hormone that helps block the production of sperm for a period of several weeks to months. Vanderbilt University Medical Center tested the contraceptive with six men who volunteered for daily injections of the drug. Researchers found no major side effects and were able to reverse sterility in the men. Scientists now are testing the effectiveness and safety of this male contraceptive in pill form.[2]

BARRIERS TO BIRTH CONTROL

The need for better contraception and broader choices in birth control methods is urgent, according to the Institute of Medicine. The Institute's recent study of reproductive health in the United States noted:

Many men and women in this country are badly informed about birth control and about the true effectiveness and health risks of the methods that are available. Half the pregnancies in this country are unintended, and the United States has one of the highest rates of abortion and teenage pregnancy among industrialized nations.... The experience of other nations suggests that to reduce the number of unintended pregnancies and abortions in this country, particularly among teenagers, we must make contraceptives more easily available and we must be more vigorous in our dissemination of information about birth control and family planning.[3]

Why aren't birth control methods and information about them readily accessible to all Americans who want or need them? One reason is the long history of political pressure to prevent the use of contraceptive devices. Some state laws that banned the sale and use of contraceptives were in effect until the 1960s.

A Connecticut law, for example, barred married couples from using contraceptives and prohibited anyone from giving information or advice about birth control devices. In 1961, the director of the Planned Parenthood League of Connecticut, part of a national group that provides information on contraceptives, gave a married couple information on birth control. State officials arrested the director, who was later convicted of violating the law. The case was upheld in an appeal to the state supreme court. But in 1965, the U.S. Supreme Court heard the case (*Griswold v. Connecticut*) and reversed the conviction, ruling that marital privacy was a fundamental right guaranteed by the Constitution; government could not interfere with that privacy.

In 1972, the Court ruled in another case (*Eisenstadt v. Baird*) that an individual, whether single or married, had the right to be free of government intrusion in such fundamental personal decisions as whether or not to procreate. The decision struck down a Massachusetts law banning the sale of contraceptives to unmarried people. With the ruling, the Court established that the right of privacy applied not only to married couples but also to individuals. People were free to make decisions about their private lives without government interference, although the Court did not declare that the right of privacy was absolute. Privacy rights, like other individual rights, have always been subject to limitations.

Today, the right to privacy is part of the volatile abortion debate that overshadows questions about contraception and disseminating information about birth control. In recent years, numerous observers have faulted both the anti- and pro-abortion groups for not putting aside their differences to make birth control more accessible. This would help prevent unwanted pregnancies and would ensure that many women would not have to face the decision of whether or not to abort.

Groups opposed to contraception have been actively involved in efforts to prevent public discussion on ways to prevent pregnancy. Such groups also oppose the use of government funds for research on new contraceptives and for pregnancy prevention programs in public institutions like schools and health clinics.

Negative attitudes about the safety and effectiveness of contraceptives also play a role in whether information about birth control is widespread. These attitudes are not necessarily tied to moral or religious views, however. Instead, people may believe that contraceptives endanger health, or they may accept myths about birth control, such as the belief that a pickle-juice douche will kill sperm or that ice cubes will freeze sperm in the vagina—methods that fail.

Some groups resist birth control information because it does not fit their cultural patterns. For example, the National Council of Negro Women and the Communications Consortium Media Center conducted a survey in 1991 on minority health issues and found that nearly 60 percent of the 1,100 women interviewed never practiced birth control. Those surveyed included African-American, Hispanic, Asian, and Indian women, and 42 percent were women in their prime child-bearing years (between eighteen and thirty-four) who never or rarely used any type of contraceptive.[4]

Although the survey did not spell out specific reasons for avoiding birth control, other studies have shown that women may refuse birth control because they may be unable or unwilling to oppose a male view of pregnancy. Males in some groups believe their manhood is being threatened if they don't "plant" children. Others simply do not like the idea of planning ahead for sexual intercourse by making provisions for pregnancy prevention. Some women believe they will be perceived as promiscuous if they use contraceptives. "My husband (boyfriend) will think I'm out running around," is a fear frequently expressed.

Information about birth control has also been stifled by

long-standing taboos against educational programs on pregnancy prevention and contraceptive advertising in the media. Many television networks refuse to run contraceptive ads because they are afraid they will offend some viewers. At the same time, however, a great number of television programs show couples having sex, and many ads suggest ways in which people can be sexually attractive. If people are encouraged by media images to be sexually active, then it would seem logical that they would also be encouraged to prevent unwanted or unplanned pregnancies.

Ironically, the ban on ads for contraceptives is easing somewhat because of the threat of sexually transmitted diseases. Some health and social service information programs in major cities have included advertising to educate the public about using condoms as protection against the human immunodeficiency virus (HIV) that causes AIDS.

The threat of AIDS has also prompted public school systems in major cities such as New York, Philadelphia, and San Francisco to set up school-based programs that provide condoms to high school students. Some parent groups and Catholic and fundamentalist Protestant religious leaders have adamantly opposed the school-based programs. They believe that distributing condoms encourages kids to have sex. But school officials and others argue that the threat of HIV infection is a matter of life and death and that students should have the means to protect themselves. Most programs require parental consent before students can participate, but in late 1991, the New York City public school system was the first to set up a program that allows students to decide for themselves whether to take part.

LIMITING TEENAGE PREGNANCIES

Birth control experts believe schools should not only distribute condoms to help prevent AIDS but should also provide sex education classes, which would include information about contraceptives, and set up contraceptive distribution through school-based health clinics. The Sex Information and Education Council of the United States (SIECUS), a nonprofit research group, reported in 1991 that nine out of ten parents want their children to have sex education in schools, but only twenty-two states require such courses.[5] Opponents contend that providing sex education and birth control information in schools encourages young people to have sex. They say educators should teach children to abstain from sexual activity and that sex education should be provided at home.

What do students think about sex education and the distribution of contraceptives in schools? In one survey of teenagers in Orange County, California, reporters found that some students favored the idea, because "teens are going to have sex anyway so why not help them do it right?" Others thought kids were "too lazy" or "too embarrassed" to buy contraceptives or could not afford them; giving out contraceptives might ensure that teenagers use them.

On the other hand, some teenagers said that providing birth control devices "condones sexual activity" or implies that sex is "casual and OK." One seventeen-year-old objected because "If I were a taxpayer I wouldn't want my money going toward someone else's good time."[6]

Other strategies that have been developed to reduce adolescent pregnancies include a "teen chastity" program set up under the federal Adolescent Family Life Act of 1981. It provides funds for secular and religious groups that are trying to encourage.young people to abstain from sex outside marriage. The program has been criticized, however, because some groups accepting federal funds use materials that contain religious messages (such as advising teenagers to "invite God on every date"). Critics maintain that federally funded materials that promote a religious view amount to government-sponsored religion, which is unconstitutional.

The Children's Defense Fund (CDF), a national group working to protect children and to improve their lives, has organized a nationwide Adolescent Pregnancy Prevention Network. Activities vary greatly, but one of the most effective projects identifies successful prevention programs and encourages network members to visit sites and see how strategies work.

Girls, Inc. (formerly Girls Clubs of America) has developed one successful program. The group's efforts include classes to teach girls between the ages of twelve and seventeen about sexuality and to help them develop assertiveness skills so that they can say no to sexual activity without losing popularity among their peers. In addition, girls learn how to make responsible decisions about contraception and how to set educational and career goals, a major factor in preventing pregnancies. Over a three-year period, Girls Inc. found that participants were much more likely to avoid sex or use birth control than those in the same age group who were not a part of the prevention program.[7]

FORCED BIRTH CONTROL?

A growing number of Americans have indicated they would like to see the contraceptive Norplant used to curb teenage pregnancy, and to help stem such social problems as poverty, drug-addicted babies, and child abuse. Just after the FDA announced approval of Norplant for use in the United States, the *Philadelphia Inquirer* published an editorial that recommended using the device to help solve the problem of poverty among a group labeled the black underclass. Although the editorial acknowledged that "more whites than blacks live in poverty," it pointed to the high percentage of poor blacks on welfare. "The main reason more black children are living in poverty is that the people having the most children are the ones least capable of supporting them," the editorial stated, adding that welfare mothers should be offered an incentive, such as increased aid payments, to use Norplant.[8]

For weeks, the editorial was a topic of heated exchanges on talk shows across the United States. Supporters in general believed that some groups of women should be required or encouraged to use Norplant in order to reduce poverty and the high costs of welfare. Those in favor of pressuring women to use contraceptives frequently made a causal link between having "too many" children and being poor.

Critics said the editorial implied that poor people should not have children, especially if the poor happened to be African-Americans. In the view of Vanessa Williams, who is on the *Inquirer* staff and is also head of the Philadelphia Association of Black Journalists, the idea was "dangerously close to state-sponsored genocide."

Williams declared the editorial position "seriously flawed" for several reasons. "It never suggested that men should share any of the responsibility for birth control [and] offered no solution to poverty, rather encouraged a pathological reliance on welfare by increasing benefits for women who agree to have the [implant]." In Williams's opinion the editorial was "an affront, not only to poor women of color, but to all reasonable, fair-minded people. It is an affront to the fundamental freedoms and rights that are guaranteed to all citizens of this country."[9]

Although incentives are used to prompt a variety of actions that appear to benefit society (such as campaigns to clean up the environment), "the line between incentive and coercion gets very fuzzy," according to Sheldon Segal, the developer of Norplant. Segal noted that when the government singles out welfare mothers, offering them a bonus not to have children, "you've gotten into a risky area, ethically and morally."[10]

The main reason for developing Norplant was to provide women with another alternative form of birth control, not to provide authorities with one more means to control women. Yet control was the emphasis of a court case in California. About the time of the *Inquirer* controversy, California Superior Court Judge Howard Broadman ordered a twenty-eight-year-old unmarried mother, Darlene Johnson, to have the birth control device implanted as a condition for probation. Otherwise she faced a prison sentence. Johnson had been convicted of brutally beating two of her four children. In his sentencing, Broadman said Johnson was not capable of caring for children and should not have others until she was emotionally prepared to do so.

The judge acknowledged the mother's right to make her own decisions about procreation. But he said that his order was justified because the state had a "compelling interest" in protecting any future children Johnson might conceive. In other words, the judge believed the state had the duty to override the mother's rights.[11]

At first Johnson agreed to the implant, but later refused the birth control device. Johnson said she did not believe in birth control and agreed to Norplant only because she feared the jail sentence. Her sentence was appealed, and a district court dismissed the case in April 1992 because it was moot—it no longer had legal significance. Since Johnson had refused to use birth control and had violated her probation, she was sentenced to five years in prison.

The court-ordered birth control has sparked an intense public debate across the nation. Opinion pieces on the subject have appeared in major newspapers, and the subject has been the topic of TV talk shows and programs such as "60 Minutes." Although some have supported the judge's decision, many others have not. In fact, several months after the birth-control sentencing, a man opposed to contraception attempted to kill the judge. Because of his close brush with death and the public criticism of his decision, Judge Broadman withdrew from the case, saying he would make no further rulings on it.

Most critics of the birth-control sentence have not faulted the judge for punishing a child abuser. The problem of child abuse is tragic, and child advocate groups across the land are trying to find ways to protect children. "But state-imposed sterilization is an irrational and unconstitutional reaction to the problem; it does nothing to help the already-existing victims of abuse," wrote attorney Helen Neuborne, executive director of the National Organization of Women's Legal Defense and Education Fund. She explained that "forced sterilization, even the temporary sterilization induced by Norplant, is not an appropriate criminal sanction in a civilized society. Depriving a human being of the fundamental right to procreate as a punishment for a crime is the hallmark of totalitarianism. We do not seriously consider forced sterilization as a punishment for any crime, even murder."[12]

Technically, Norplant is not considered a sterilization procedure since a woman is fertile once the hormone capsules are removed. But forced birth control is repugnant to those who see it as a form of state-sponsored eugenics. In other words, enforced birth control suggests trying to improve the population by eliminating people considered "undesirable." This raises the specter of Hitler's attempts to try to create a "super race" of Germans, eliminating all who did not fit what he determined was the ideal model. Hitler's Nazis sterilized hundreds of thousands of people with disabilities as well as killing millions of Jewish people and other minorities who were labeled "subhuman" and "degenerate."

The idea of ridding society of unwanted people has not been confined to Nazi Germany, however. During the early 1900s in the United States, all states required sterilization of the mentally disabled, and most states did not allow the "feeble minded" to marry. Although these laws have been overturned for the most part, it is not unusual today for people with disabilities to be pressured to accept "voluntary" sterilization. In addition, there have been numerous cases documented during the past few decades in which girls and women of color have been sterilized without their knowledge, frequently in connection with childbirth or abortion.[13]

In spite of the dangers of government coercion in reproductive matters, a *Los Angeles Times* poll of more than 1,600 Californians found that 61 percent of the respondents approved of making Norplant mandatory for drug-abusing women of child-bearing age. Of that number, 46 percent "strongly approved" of such measures, and 15 percent said they "approved somewhat." Only 32 percent were against the idea of forced birth control for drug addicts.[14]

Chapter
Four

DEBATES OVER FETAL "PERSONHOOD" AND ABORTION

While contraception and birth control are controversial issues in the United States, they do not create as much discord and debate as the issue of elective or deliberate abortion—terminating a pregnancy by surgical or medicinal means. Arguments do not focus on spontaneous abortions, usually called miscarriages, in which a woman's body, for biological reasons or because of injury or disease, rejects a fetus.

Elective abortions are legal, within limits, and nationwide polls have shown consistently that the majority of Americans favors a woman's right to an abortion. However, the polls have also shown that many individuals want abortions to be limited, and that some people are adamantly opposed to abortion and want it banned entirely.[1]

Abortion arguments usually stem from conflicting views on when life begins and whether or not a fetus is a person and has rights equal to that of someone already born. On one side are those who believe that life (and thus "personhood") begins at conception, when the male sperm fertilizes the female egg and becomes a single-celled organism (known as a zygote in medical terminology). According to this view, the zygote is an unborn person and terminating a pregnancy by abortion is akin to murder. On the other side are those who argue that all life, including human life, is part of a continuum that has been in progress for eons and is constantly evolving. Therefore the question is not when does life begin but when does the fetus become a person? Based on this view, personhood may begin when the fetus is viable, or able to live outside the womb, and has the potential to continue the life process.

WHAT IS FETAL PERSONHOOD?

Many sociologists and anthropologists point out that any definition of personhood depends on the culture and circumstances of each society. Some societies do not consider a child a person until well after birth—perhaps at six days or six months or six years. The day a child is named or some other ceremonial event may be the time when an infant or young child is actually accepted as a person and part of the cultural group.

In the United States, concepts of when a fetus becomes a person are based not only on social customs but also on religious beliefs, scientific and medical findings, and legal opinions —all of which are controversial. For example, the Catholic Church and many evangelistic Protestant churches believe that human life begins at conception and that any deliberate actions that harm the developing fetus are immoral and should be illegal. But many other religious groups maintain that doctrines claiming a fetus is a person from conception are based on personal interpretations of biblical teachings; no clear-cut biblical codes exist on these reproductive matters.

As scientists have gained more knowledge about the fetus, they in turn have developed varied opinions about fetal personhood. Some medical researchers, for example, declare a fetus is an actual person, because from the time an egg is fertilized, the zygote that results contains the genetic material that creates a unique human life. Once conception takes place, a distinct entity—a human being—has been formed, therefore that entity should be treated as a potential person entitled to legal protection.

While few argue that a zygote can become a human being, that possibility does not make the zygote or the later embryo or fetus a person, according to many scientists. Neurologists (those who specialize in functions of the human nervous system) say that without a functioning brain a person does not exist. After conception, the human brain takes many months to develop, so the personhood of a fetus cannot begin until about the seventh month. Neurologists refute the argument that the presence of brain waves in a six-week-old fetus is proof that a "person" exists. Electrical activity is common in nearly all human cells, even those in a test tube. A fetus can respond automatically to stimuli, like amoebas or like people in a vegetative state whose reactions are not controlled by the brain because the brain is "dead." Brain waves in a fetus are not meaningful until about thirty weeks.[2]

Yet no one can provide an absolute, biological definition of what personhood is or show when personhood begins or ends. Personhood "is a value judgment that . . . society makes about a being," according to Marjorie Reiley Maguire, a Catholic theologian who does not agree with the official Catholic Church stance that human life begins at conception. What makes a person, in Maguire's view, is "relatedness to others" and membership in the human community.

"My position is that the only way a fetus can become a member of the human community, and therefore a person, prior to birth, is if the woman in whose body it exists welcomes it into the human community by her consent to the pregnancy," Maguire stated. She cautioned that there is "no neat moment that marks the dividing line between non-person and person" in the real experiences of pregnant women. Those who accept a pregnancy may immediately think of a fetus as a person; those who do not may think of a fetus as a biological object.[3]

People who believe that a fetus is a person also believe that a fetus has the "right to life" and should be protected by law. Although the fetus has some limited rights, no U.S. laws regard the unborn as "whole persons" with rights equal to those who are born. However, in recent years court cases have established an increasing number of rights and higher legal status for the fetus.

For example, in some states a person who causes an automobile accident that results in the death of a pregnant woman can also be charged with the death of the fetus. If a pregnant woman suffers injuries in an accident and her child is born with physical injuries or brain damage, the child can sue the person responsible for the injuries. In other cases, pregnant women who have been seriously injured or have developed life-threatening diseases have been kept alive against their expressed wishes because judges have ruled that the fetus must be saved. Government officials have also forced pregnant women to have blood transfusions or other medical treatment considered necessary for the well-being of the fetus.

EARLY ABORTION LAWS

Fetal personhood and fetal rights are passionately debated today, but these concepts gained little public attention until the U.S. Supreme Court ruled in 1973 to legalize a woman's right to choose an abortion. For a century before that decision, most states strictly regulated and severely restricted abortion.

Nonetheless, from colonial days to about the time of the Civil War, abortion was *not* a legal offense. In fact, only common (unwritten) law governed abortion. It was generally accepted that women should be able to abort before quickening, or the time of the first movements of the fetus in the womb. But early in the 1800s, some Americans began expressing alarm over the falling birth rate among white Anglo-Saxon Protestants, or people of northern European ancestry. During that period, many young children died in infancy and in early childhood, and an increasing number of women in this dominant group were having abortions. Leaders of the so-called ruling class feared that their group would be outnumbered by the rapidly increasing immigrants of other religious, national, and racial backgrounds. As a result, they initiated efforts to restrict abortion through state laws.

The American Medical Association (AMA) also joined the campaign to ban abortions, citing the need to prevent deaths and injuries from abortions performed by unlicensed practitioners. Even when licensed doctors performed abortions, the AMA warned, physicians could not effectively prevent infections or stop dangerous excessive bleeding after an abortion. (At the time, doctors did not have access to the kinds of antiseptics, antibiotics, or other medications available today.)

In 1821, Connecticut passed the first state law to make abortion after quickening a criminal offense. Seven years later, New York adopted a law that many other states used as a model banning abortions at any time unless they were necessary to save a pregnant woman's life. Although New York and several other states later legalized abortion during the early 1970s, most states maintained strict abortion laws. These were in effect until Norma McCorvey, a twenty-year-old Dallas, Texas woman, won a test case before the U.S. Supreme Court.

In 1970, McCorvey had been denied an abortion because it was illegal in Texas except to save the life of a pregnant woman. McCorvey, who was single and working only occasionally at low-paying jobs, had no resources to care for a child. But she was forced to continue an unwanted pregnancy and release her child for adoption, never being allowed to learn whether her child was a son or daughter.

While making adoption arrangements, McCorvey discovered that civil rights lawyers were planning to challenge the Texas law and needed someone to file a lawsuit. She agreed to be that person. To protect her privacy, lawyers named her Jane Roe in the lawsuit.

ROE V. WADE AND THE AFTERMATH

In 1973, the U.S. Supreme Court justices heard the case, *Roe v. Wade*, and in their decision struck down all state laws that severely restricted abortion. They established instead national criteria that allowed pregnant women to choose, with virtually no restrictions, to abort during the first trimester, or the first three months of pregnancy. The High Court ruled that the state (government) had an interest in protecting a pregnant woman's health and toward that end could impose regulations on abortion procedures during the second trimester. During the third trimester, when the fetus is viable, the state's interest in protecting potential human life allowed government to ban abortion unless necessary to protect the health and life of the pregnant woman.

Justice Harry Blackmun, who wrote the majority decision, pointed out that "mortality rates for women undergoing early abortions, where the procedure is legal, appear to be as low as or lower than the rates for normal childbirth. Consequently, any interest of the state in protecting the woman from an inherently hazardous procedure, except when it would be equally dangerous for her to forgo it, has largely disappeared." But the justice added that the state had a strong interest "in regulating the conditions under which abortions are performed ... and in protecting prenatal life."

Although the majority opinion acknowledged various religious and ethical views about whether or not life begins at conception, the Court noted that "those trained in the respective disciplines of medicine, philosophy, and theology are unable to arrive at any consensus, [so] the judiciary at this point... is not in a position to speculate as to the answer." In short, the state's interest in protecting fetal life could not be based on any religious view regarding when life begins. Instead, the state should take into account the biological development of the fetus, particularly after viability, "because the fetus then presumably has the capability of meaningful life outside the mother's womb."

An important part of the *Roe v. Wade* decision was based on individual privacy rights as guaranteed by the Constitution. In determining whether a woman could legally choose abortion, Justice Blackmun said the right of privacy as spelled out in various amendments, particularly the Fourteenth Amendment, must be considered. "This right of privacy... is broad enough to encompass a woman's decision whether or not to terminate a pregnancy," the Court determined.

Of course, no right is absolute, including the right to privacy. And the Court held that a pregnant woman's right to privacy should be limited as the fetus developed. A woman could legally choose to abort a pregnancy up to about twenty-four to twenty-eight weeks after conception, and at any time when her health or life was at stake.[4]

Since the *Roe v. Wade* decision, many anti-abortion groups have challenged the ruling—both in and out of courts. Over the years numerous anti-abortion protest groups have conducted stormy demonstrations in order to call attention to their cause. Some send hate mail, vandalize property, and harass and threaten families of doctors who perform abortions. Others have trashed or bombed clinics, threatening people's lives while demanding the "right to life" for the unborn.

Violence escalated in 1993. In March, David Gunn, a doctor working in a Florida abortion clinic, was murdered by an abortion foe who claimed he acted in the name of God. During the summer, a doctor who performed abortions in Wichita, Kansas, was shot in both arms by an Oregon woman who had taken part in numerous anti-abortion rallies across the country. A few days later, George Patterson, a doctor and owner of abortion clinics in Florida and Alabama, was shot dead. Although investigators were not sure whether Patterson's murder was committed by an anti-abortionist, an anti-abortion group in Pensacola, Florida, issued a statement to the media saying that if the assailant was motivated by "an anti-abortion mind-set," the assault was "justifiable" because "[o]ne less person is killing preborn children and four abortion clinics are closed."[5]

David Trosch, a Catholic priest of Magnolia Springs, Alabama, had made similar public statements a few days earlier during a radio program interview, prompting scores of listeners to call in with angry protests. Trosch also tried to place a newspaper ad showing a man pointing a gun at a doctor about to perform an abortion, with the heading "Justifiable homicide." Two newspapers refused the ad. Eventually, church officials disavowed the priest's comments as contrary to Roman Catholic teachings and ordered Trosch to recant his statements.

Many other Americans also have denounced those who say that differences in beliefs justify one person killing another. Although some fear that this intolerant attitude and violence will continue, many anti-abortionists work within the legal system. Some have formed political groups to pressure for state laws limiting abortion.

Missouri, for example, passed a law that begins with a preamble stating that "the life of each human being begins at conception" and directing its legislature to interpret Missouri laws so that unborn children are provided with the same rights as people already born. The law forbids the use of public funds for abortions—that is, abortions cannot be performed in public hospitals and clinics or in private facilities located on land rented from the government. (In Missouri, 97 percent of all abortions after sixteen weeks of pregnancy are performed in a private hospital located on government land, thus the law effectively forbids abortion for a great many women.) Another major provision of the law requires a woman to undergo medical tests to determine the viability of the fetus after twenty weeks.

In 1988, a family planning facility challenged the Missouri law, and a federal appeals court declared it unconstitutional. But in 1989, the Missouri attorney general appealed the case before the U.S. Supreme Court (*Webster v. Reproductive Health Services*), and the majority of the justices upheld the Missouri law, although they did not rule on the preamble, calling it a philosophical statement with no legal power to regulate abortions.

After the *Webster* decision, people from all parts of the United States and many walks of life spoke out in opposition to or in support of the ruling. Many who opposed the ruling believed the Court had, in effect, placed the state's interest in protecting the fetus over a woman's right to determine whether she should have an abortion. Critics also argued that restrictions on abortion pit women's rights against the rights of the fetus. No matter who or what determines when the fetus is viable, the fetus should not have rights equal to that of a person already born, opponents declared.

John C. Wilke, then president of the National Right to Life Committee, called the decision "historic" and a ruling that would begin "the process of restoring a fundamental right to the American people—the right to protect human life." Others, such as then U.S. Attorney General Richard Thornburgh, said the decision was welcome because it recognized "an increased role for state legislatures in regulating abortion." He added that "those of us opposed to abortion on demand can take heart that a majority of the justices have seen fit to give the states greater leeway in establishing appropriate limitations on abortion."[6]

Indeed, since the *Webster* ruling, several states have passed laws that ban the use of public funds to pay for abortions, require waiting periods before an abortion can be performed, and require pregnant teenagers to obtain parental consent before they can have an abortion. Although proponents of the parental consent law claim that such legislation has slowed the rate of teenage abortions, opponents say the laws contribute to terrible dilemmas.

In one case, an Indianapolis, Indiana, teenager who did not want to hurt her parents by informing them that she was pregnant went to an illegal abortionist, suffered an infection, and died. The girl's parents have since been campaigning to overturn the parental consent law and to maintain legalized abortion.

In another instance, a fifteen-year-old Michigan girl became pregnant after a gang rape and asked the state's Department of Social Services to pay the $1,000 fee for an abortion because she and her family did not have the money for the procedure. The agency refused because of a state ban on the use of public funds for abortion, but anonymous donors who had heard of the girl's plight came to her rescue. Later, the Michigan chapter of the American Civil Liberties Union (ACLU) filed a lawsuit on the girl's behalf. The Michigan Court of Appeals struck down the funding ban, ruling that the equal protection clause in the state constitution guarantees that all women should have access to abortion services, even those whose health services are paid for with government funds.

Over the past few years, Louisiana, Pennsylvania, and Utah have passed legislation that bans most abortions except when pregnancies are the result of incest or rape or when a woman's health or life is endangered. Pro-choice groups attacked these statutes, calling them unconstitutional, and appealed to the Supreme Court to determine whether the legislation violated constitutional rights. Many wanted the Court to determine once and for all whether provisions of *Roe v. Wade* would stand.

Chapter
Five

OTHER
ABORTION-
RELATED ISSUES

Since the 1980s, arguments over legal restrictions on abortion have continued unabated, but the public controversy has broadened to include other abortion-related issues. One was the debate over a federal regulation, dubbed a "gag rule," that forbade counseling on abortion at any family planning service accepting federal funds. Other issues included the FDA's ban on the import and development of RU-486, and the federal ban on use of tissue from aborted fetuses to treat serious diseases.

THE GAG RULE

Because of pressure from anti-abortion groups, President Ronald Reagan initiated the gag rule in 1988, but the regulation was not implemented until late 1992. The regulation prohibited the distribution of federal funds to facilities that counseled their clients on abortion or referred them to abortion clinics. These facilities included state health departments, public hospital clinics in big cities, community health services in rural areas, and Planned Parenthood clinics. Many pro-choice organizations, the League of Women Voters, and medical groups joined in a lawsuit to prevent enforcement of the gag rule, calling it an infringement of privacy and free speech rights. But a U.S. Court of Appeals upheld the regulation.

Again the ruling was appealed. Then in 1991, the U.S. Supreme Court heard the case (*Rust v. Sullivan*) and declared the gag rule constitutional.

Some family planning clinics said they would forgo the federal funds, which they called "hush money," rather than remain silent about abortion. One Portland, Maine, counselor told *The New York Times* that "If I have a sixteen-year-old girl with an alcohol problem who's living on the streets and finds out she's pregnant, or the twelve-year-old I saw last week who was sexually abused by her stepfather, and they ask me about abortion, how could I possibly say I can't answer their questions? It would be abandoning my responsibility to them."[1]

Polly Hay, a nurse who managed the emergency room of a New Jersey hospital and made a series of TV commercials opposing the gag rule, wrote in a nationally distributed opinion piece that the regulation violated "the most fundamental medical ethics." One of the basic responsibilities of health care professionals is providing the best possible information on health care so that patients can make educated decisions about their treatment. But in Hay's opinion, the gag rule prevented "patients from making their own decisions. For patients facing almost every disease or condition, medical professionals can spell out options and speak freely. But if a woman is pregnant, the government wants to act like Big Brother and censor the conversation."[2]

As criticism mounted, President George Bush announced in March 1992 that the ruling would be modified so that doctors could discuss abortion with their patients, but nurses and other health care workers would have to abide by the gag rule. However, the modification still infringed on free speech rights, many people believed, and family planning groups began pressuring Congress to abolish the regulation. In January 1993, two days after his inauguration, President Clinton reversed the executive order that established the gag rule. This reversal did not include changes in laws forbidding federal funding for abortions. But another Clinton executive order overturned a restriction on abortions in military hospitals overseas. Although federal funds cannot be used, patients who pay for their own abortions are no longer prohibited from having an abortion in military hospitals, which are sometimes the only safe places for performing an abortion.

PLANNED PARENTHOOD V. CASEY

In July 1992, the U.S. Supreme Court delivered another important decision that has placed more restrictions on abortion. The case (*Planned Parenthood of Southeastern Pennsylvania v. Casey*) made its way to the High Court after Pennsylvania Governor Robert P. Casey signed a restrictive abortion law in 1990.

One provision of the Pennsylvania law required pregnant women seeking an abortion to wait twenty-four hours in order to think over their decision before being allowed to end a pregnancy. Other provisions required pregnant married women to notify their husbands, and minors under age eighteen to obtain parental consent to have an abortion. The law also stipulated that doctors must provide women with information packets about abortion, including descriptions of fetal development, the risks of abortion, and alternatives to abortion.

Not long after the law was passed, a federal district court found the statute unconstitutional, but Pennsylvania appealed the decision, and an appellate court upheld the state law. Attorneys for Planned Parenthood and other pro-choice groups then petitioned the Supreme Court to take the case. After hearing the case, the High Court in June 1992 ruled that most of the Pennsylvania law could stand but declared the spousal notification provision unconstitutional, because it placed an "undue burden" on married women seeking an abortion.

The Court recognized that many married women feared physical abuse from their husbands if they were required to notify them of a planned abortion. In a joint opinion written by Justices Sandra Day O'Connor, Anthony M. Kennedy, and

David H. Souter, the Court stated that "Constitutional protection of the woman's decision to terminate her pregnancy derives from the Due Process Clause of the Fourteenth Amendment.... It is a promise of the Constitution that there is a realm of personal liberty which the government may not enter.... It is settled now, as it was when the Court heard arguments in Roe v. Wade, that the Constitution places limits on a State's right to interfere with a person's most basic decisions about family and parenthood."

The justices declared that their opinion was also based on precedents established by previous Courts. If decisions were made without taking precedent into account, "the Court's legitimacy" and "the Nation's commitment to the rule of law" could be severely damaged, the Court stated.

Although the justices upheld basic elements of *Roe v. Wade*, they replaced the trimester framework of that decision with the "undue burden" test as a means of determining whether a law is constitutional. "An undue burden exists, and a provision of a law is invalid if its purpose or effect is to place a substantial obstacle in the path of a woman seeking an abortion before the fetus attains viability," the justices wrote.[3]

However, no one is sure how lower court judges will apply the "undue burden" requirement if state lawmakers pass more restrictive abortion laws, which both pro-choice and anti-abortion advocates are convinced will happen. Because of this uncertainty, a few states have already enacted laws or are attempting to pass statutes that maintain most of the provisions guaranteed by *Roe v. Wade*.

PREPARING FOR STATE RESTRICTIONS

If abortion is severely restricted in some states, what steps will women who want to terminate an unwanted pregnancy take? Some may travel elsewhere for the procedure, even out of the country, which was common before 1973. But traveling a long distance from home for an abortion can be expensive, so those most likely to take this action will be those who can afford to pay the costs. Most poor women, as is often the case today, will be forced to carry an unwanted pregnancy to term, which many pro-choice advocates say makes women mandatory childbearers, not much different from chattel, or slaves.

Prior to *Roe*, a nationwide network of clergy helped thousands of women go from their home state to another—usually New York or California—for legal abortions. Religious leaders may initiate such a practice again if states restrict abortions. Already, the Quakers, or Friends, have set up a nationwide network that will help women with housing and transportation if they must travel from state to state to legally terminate an unwanted pregnancy.

Although Quakers generally oppose abortion, the plans for an "overground railroad" for pregnant women are in the Quaker tradition. Before the Civil War, the Quakers operated the underground railroad, helping slaves travel from the south to freedom in northern states. Trish Walach, cofounder of the network, says "Freedom has always been a very important part of being a Quaker, and the freedom to choose to have an abortion or to continue a pregnancy is very basic."[4]

Women's rights advocates believe that some women who want to terminate a pregnancy will try self-induced abortions, just as women have always done. This triggers images of women inserting coat hangers or other objects into the uterus or of sleazy back-alley abortionists. But women may use a self-help procedure known as menstrual extraction, which was widely practiced during the 1960s and 1970s before legal abortions in medical clinics were available. Interest in the procedure has resurfaced as more and more women seek advice about how to provide abortions for each other should they need to do so. According to women's health centers, well-trained practitioners can perform the extraction safely with a minimum of equipment in the privacy of a woman's own home.

Still, some abortion rights groups are concerned about the safety of self-induced abortions and believe that more attention must be given to such projects as electing pro-choice legislators and passing a Freedom of Choice Act—a federal law to ensure a woman's right to abortion. Many proponents of the proposed legislation believe it will prevent further constitutional challenges to abortion rights. Pro-choice groups, along with medical and scientific groups, also have worked to have the so-called abortion pill, RU-486, tested in the United States.

THE RU-486 CONTROVERSY

RU-486 is designed to induce menstrual bleeding during the first seven weeks after conception. The drug stimulates a woman's body chemistry and prompts the uterus to shed its lining and embryo. It causes a condition similar to a spontaneous miscarriage, nature's way of aborting an embryo that is less than an inch long and in no way resembles anything like a person. Data on tens of thousands of European women who have taken the drug show that it has one of the highest ratings for safe, nonsurgical abortions. In addition, it has been successfully used in Europe to treat breast cancer, one type of brain tumor, and endometriosis (a cause of infertility). European doctors say the drug helps women who have difficulty in labor to give birth vaginally, reducing the number of Caesarean deliveries.[5]

Because the U.S. Food and Drug Administration banned private use of the drug, only medical scientists could import the drug for study. Private citizens were prohibited from bringing the pills into the United States, even though the FDA allowed the import of other unapproved medicinal drugs for compassionate reasons—that is, to treat diseases that have no known cure or effective antidote. In 1990, the FDA declared that RU-486 did not fall under the exception. But pro-choice advocates argued that a pregnant woman who wanted an abortion was entitled to compassion. In addition, many members of Congress and medical research groups said the FDA action was strictly political. Even some FDA officials admitted that the ban on RU-486 was politically motivated.

There is no doubt that anti-abortion groups consistently pressured members of Congress and President George Bush and his administration to prohibit the drug's use. The National Right to Life Committee and others opposed to abortion threatened boycotts of all U.S. companies that might attempt to manufacture and sell RU-486 in the United States. "We have told them that the day a license application is made for this drug in the United States, all hell will break loose.... We don't want that human pesticide in the United States," said John C. Willke, then president of the National Right to Life Committee.[6] As a result, European manufacturers, who feared the adverse publicity and threats from anti-abortion groups, refused to release the drug for export to the United States.

Nevertheless, efforts continued to overturn the FDA ban on RU-486. Women's groups like the Feminist Majority Foundation (FMF) planned to bring together small U.S. pharmaceutical companies to research and develop possible alternatives to RU-486. An alternative plan was to raise funds to form a feminist-controlled drug company "that would put research for women's health first, the bottom line second, and indeed would never play politics with women's lives," according to Eleanor Smeal, president of the foundation.[7]

In September 1991, Peg Yorkin, a TV producer and cofounder of the FMF, donated $10 million to the foundation so that part of the funds could be used in a campaign to pressure the U.S. Food and Drug Administration to allow testing of the drug. The group also launched efforts to convince French and German manufacturers of RU-486 to try to market the drug in the United States.

The first lawsuit challenging the FDA ban was initiated during the summer of 1992. A pregnant California woman, Leona Benten, with the support of several pro-choice groups, deliberately set the stage for the court case. Benten went to England to fill a prescription from her physician for RU-486 and returned to the United States with a single dose of the drug. Pro-choice groups alerted U.S. Customs agents that Benten would be arriving at Kennedy Airport in New York with RU-486, anticipating that reporters would cover the event. To publicize her challenge, Benten planned to ingest the pill at the airport, but customs agents detained her and confiscated the drug.

A few days later, Benten, along with a newly formed group called the Center for Reproductive Law and Policy, filed a class action lawsuit in a U.S. district court in New York to prevent the FDA from enforcing the import ban on RU-486 and to return the drug to Benten. The lawsuit charged that the FDA had acted illegally, prohibiting the import of RU-486 for political reasons, and that Benten would suffer harm if she could not take the pill. Although a federal judge ruled in Benten's favor, the case was immediately appealed by the U.S. Justice Department with the support of the Bush administration. A U.S. appeals court reversed the ruling of the lower court. Benten appealed to the U.S. Supreme Court, but the justices ruled in favor of the FDA import ban. Because of the decision, Benten had a surgical abortion.[8]

In 1993, when President Clinton rescinded the ban on the import of RU-486, subject to FDA approval, he pointed out in a news conference that the FDA ban had been imposed because of "factors other than an assessment of the possible health and safety risks of the drug." He ordered the FDA to assess the drug on those factors alone. FDA Commissioner David A. Kessler promised immediate evaluation of RU-486, although he did not predict when the results would be available.

DEBATES OVER FETAL TISSUE TRANSPLANTS

Just as RU-486 use became part of the rancorous abortion battle so did the use of fetal tissue for transplants. In a fetal tissue transplant, surgeons transplant cells from aborted fetuses (those between the sixth and eleventh weeks of gestation) in patients and in effect reconstruct defective "parts," rather like mechanics repair cars or machinery. During the 1980s, for example, neurosurgeons in several countries, including Sweden, Mexico, China, and Canada, transplanted fetal tissue into the brains of people suffering from Parkinson's disease, an incurable disorder that destroys nerve cells in the brain. The destroyed nerve cells prevent the release of a chemical called dopamine, which transmits messages from one part of the brain to another, and eventually Parkinson's patients lose their ability to control movement and speech. Transplanted fetal brain cells help produce dopamine in Parkinson's patients. About 100 victims of the disease worldwide have shown some improvement after transplants.

Surgeons have also transplanted tissue from fetal pancreases in patients with diabetes, a disease that affects the ability to produce insulin, which is needed to process carbohydrates and glucose (sugar) in the bloodstream. Implanted cells grow quickly and prompt the patient's pancreas to produce natural insulin, which helps a diabetic control blood sugar and improves overall health.

Researchers say fetal tissue transplants can also help victims of Alzheimer's disease, another serious brain disorder, and many other ailments. But until 1993, the only transplants of fetal tissue allowed in the United States were those paid for with private funds. During the administration of President Ronald Reagan, top government officials, pressured by anti-abortion groups, banned the use of federal funds for experiments with fetal tissue. The administration of President George Bush continued the ban, even though legal experts in the Health and Human Services Administration said the ban was illegal.

In one more reversal of previous government policy, President Clinton lifted the ban on federal funding of fetal tissue research, which, many medical experts believe, should encourage more private research in fetal tissue transplants. Before the reversal, private foundations and drug companies were reluctant to support such research because of the federal government's prohibition and what some researchers believed was political intervention in scientific research.

Yet there are still many vocal foes of fetal tissue transplants who believe that even though the procedure can help people with debilitating diseases, the social and moral costs are too high. Basically, opponents say if fetal tissue transplants become commonplace, they will make abortion appear beneficial and thus encourage more elective abortions. Anti-abortionists, however, do not generally oppose the use of tissue from a fetus removed because of a tubal pregnancy (the embryo is implanted outside the uterus in the fallopian tubes—a life-threatening condition) or other surgery required to save the life of the pregnant woman.

Not all opponents of fetal tissue transplants are anti-abortionists. Some accept legalized abortion and favor fetal research but oppose the use of fetal tissue if women opt to have an abortion for the sole purpose of treating a disabling disease. News reports over the past few years have described several instances in which women have expressed their willingness to conceive and abort a fetus in order to help a relative or friend with a disease like Parkinson's.

In some ways, the idea is similar to bearing a child to serve as a tissue or an organ donor, a practice that occurs on a fairly regular basis, although it is seldom discussed or acknowledged. Recently, however, a California couple, Abe and Mary Ayala, publicized their decision to have a child in order to provide a compatible donor for their daughter, Marissa, a leukemia victim who needed a bone marrow transplant. The Ayalas felt their decision was ethical because it saved another's life. But some doctors, ethicists, and others argue that parents might decide to abort fetuses that do not have the tissue type needed by donor recipients, which would be ethically unacceptable to many in our society. They also feel uncomfortable with what they believe is having a baby as a means to an end, rather than valuing the child as an individual.

No one expects any of the social, political, and moral controversies revolving around fetal tissue transplants, or any other abortion issues for that matter, to be resolved soon. Even people who adamantly oppose abortion may heartily endorse a fetal tissue transplant if it saves the life of their child or other close relative. Each situation requires decisions based on a person's own beliefs and values, which is the basic argument of those who support the fundamental right of a woman to choose an abortion.

Chapter
Six

THE IMPACT
OF MEDICAL
TECHNOLOGY ON
REPRODUCTIVE
CHOICES

While terminating and preventing pregnancy receive the most widespread attention, issues surrounding conception and giving birth are also part of public discussions on human reproduction. New medical technologies (NRTs) have changed the way women become pregnant and give birth. These technologies include artificial means of conception using procedures to fertilize an egg outside a woman's body and an increasing number of new methods to monitor fetal health.

NRTs have generated many questions about who controls childbearing decisions. Some women's health advocates and feminist groups insist that as the medical community increasingly uses technology to intervene in childbearing, scientists and physicians—intentionally or unwittingly—manipulate women to accept practices that may not be in their best interests. Others take the opposite view, saying NRTs allow women to choose among a number of alternatives when they are making decisions about procreation.

ARTIFICIAL INSEMINATION

The earliest form of intervention in human reproduction began more than 200 years ago when researchers successfully inseminated (impregnated) animals by artificial means. These scientists discussed the possibility of humans conceiving by methods other than sexual intercourse, and physicians applied their theories, experimenting with artificial insemination as a way to treat human infertility, or the inability to reproduce. Since then, many couples who previously had not been able to conceive have been able to do so through a relatively simple artificial procedure.

In most instances today, the procedure is performed by a doctor who deposits semen from a woman's husband or other donor in a small cap that fits over the cervix, or places it in a syringe and deposits sperm directly into the vagina. A person without medical expertise can perform the procedure, but nearly half of U.S. states have passed laws requiring a physician to perform artificial insemination by a donor. One reason for such laws is to ensure appropriate screening to prevent the spread of venereal diseases and genetic disorders through donated sperm.

Married couples are the primary users of artificial insemination, but single women without male partners may want the procedure as well. However, because of social customs and religious beliefs, many Americans object to single women or women in nonstandard relationships (for example, lesbian couples) having children. Thus doctors may deny insemination to single women. They also may refuse to perform the procedure for couples who belong to religious groups that forbid the practice.

Some women, however, have objected to medical control over their reproductive decisions and have practiced self-insemination. They have been able to impregnate themselves by using a simple kitchen utensil (a turkey baster) or a syringe that contains semen purchased from a sperm bank (a laboratory where sperm is preserved).

While the practice of artificially depositing sperm in the vagina to impregnate a woman is a relatively simple matter, other types of artificial conception require the use of laboratory techniques and medical intervention to bring about a pregnancy. Such technology started with in vitro (in glass) fertilization.

IN VITRO FERTILIZATION

During the 1960s and 1970s, researchers conducted experiments with in vitro fertilization (IVF), placing ovum, or egg, and sperm in a glass container called a petri dish so that the ovum could be fertilized. Once the zygote was created, a doctor was able to place it in a woman's body to develop as in a normal pregnancy. But it was not until 1978 that the procedure proved successful. In July of that year, Louise Brown was born—the world's first "test-tube baby" as she was called, although she was conceived with IVF procedures.

Since the 1970s, scientists have developed a variety of IVF techniques that have been used to produce thousands of American babies. Nearly 16,000 babies were born between 1987 and 1992 as a result of IVF and related procedures according to the American Fertility Society, based in Birmingham, Alabama.[1]

Who are the consumers of the new reproductive technology? Some are women who have waited until their thirties or forties to try to conceive. Beyond about age thirty-five, women have more difficulty conceiving than they might have had during their earlier and more fertile years. In addition, fertility specialists have been able to help women have children after menopause, when the ovulation cycle stops. Women beyond the age of forty may undergo hormone therapy to help the uterus accept an implanted embryo created through IVF techniques. As a result, some have been able to experience healthy pregnancies.

Others who use artificial means to procreate are men or women who are infertile due to sexually transmitted diseases or because of adverse reactions to prescribed medications and illegal drugs. Alcoholism and exposure to toxic chemicals in the workplace can also lead to infertility.

An increasing number of people, who spend from $6,000 to over $50,000 for services, are seeking help with infertility at IVF infertility centers or clinics. Only a few such centers existed in the United States before the 1980s. Today there are well over 200 IVF facilities nationwide, where, as a *Time* magazine report noted, "Doctors today can manipulate virtually every aspect of the reproductive cycle, from artificially ripening eggs in the ovary to inserting individual sperm directly into the egg's inner membrane."[2]

One of the basic procedures doctors use in IVF is prescribing drugs—hormones—for women to stimulate the production of more than one mature egg during the ovulation cycle. With multiple eggs to fertilize, there is a better chance of producing a healthy embryo for implantation.

In recent years, fertility experts have tailored IVF procedures in processes known as GIFT and ZIFT. GIFT is the acronym for gamete intra-fallopian transfer. A doctor inserts unfertilized eggs and sperm into a woman's fallopian tube, where fertilization may take place. In ZIFT, a variation on GIFT, the egg is fertilized in a petri dish and the resulting zygote is placed in the fallopian tube. Another variation is microinjection, in which the sperm is injected into the egg with a thin needle. Zona drilling is still one more technique. A hole is made in the egg's protective shell to allow the sperm to penetrate. If any of the procedures is successful and the embryo is implanted, a woman may be able to continue her pregnancy to term.

Yet many people ask: Where is all this "high-tech" reproduction leading? For infertile couples the answer might be "to a miracle" or "to an indescribably wonderful experience," as some have said. One woman who at forty-one years of age had given up hope of ever having children, was able to reproduce with an implanted embryo created from her husband's sperm and another woman's egg. The mother said her experience was "the biggest thrill of our lives!...I would tell any woman in my situation to go for it. Absolutely!"[3]

On the other hand, the new reproductive technology has

been applied in ways that create ethical, political, and legal dilemmas. For example, it is now possible to freeze embryos in liquid nitrogen in a process called cryopreservation. Some scientists hail this procedure because if an implant fails, another embryo can be used without subjecting a woman to the lengthy and rigorous IVF cycle. But problems may arise over what to do with frozen embryos if a couple moves away, divorces, or dies.

In one case, a wealthy couple who had frozen embryos in storage was killed in a plane crash. A judge ordered that the embryos had to be thawed and implanted in a woman who would bring them to term, if such a woman could be found. Then the children born would have to be placed for adoption.

In a widely publicized 1989 case, Junior Lewis Davis and Mary Sue Davis of Maryville, Tennessee, filed for a no-fault divorce, which might have been settled quickly except for complex legal dilemmas over the fate of their frozen embryos. Through IVF procedures, using her eggs and his sperm, the Davises produced seven embryos, which were frozen and stored at a medical center in Knoxville. Mary Davis wanted possession of the embryos in order to have them implanted at a later date. Junior Davis no longer wanted children and did not want any embryo produced with his sperm implanted in any woman.

During the divorce trial many complex issues arose: Should the embryos be considered jointly owned property to be evenly divided? Should one of the partners receive custody of the embryos? Should the medical center hold the embryos in storage for implantation at a much later date in another woman? Should the embryos be discarded? Should they be donated to another couple?

The judge in the Davis case eventually awarded "custody" of the embryos to Mary Davis, ruling that "human life begins at conception." Yet the abortion controversy has shown that the question of when life begins has never been resolved in absolute scientific or legal terms. The judge's decision did little to answer the myriad questions about the status of frozen embryos, and many legal experts, bioethicists (those who study moral issues raised when new biological techniques are used), religious leaders, and civil rights activists are still debating this issue.

Some criticize embryo freezing, saying the practice is just one more step in downgrading women while raising the status of the embryo. Others argue whether the embryo is a prospective person, requiring protection by government, or a product with high market value. Since frozen embryos can be implanted in women who have no genetic connection, many are concerned about the commercialization of the process. Clinics already recruit women for reproductive services, paying them to donate eggs to help create embryos in the laboratory or to use their uteruses to develop embryos so that others can have children. The question then is: are the women being exploited or are they simply providing a benevolent service for part of the society?

"EGG DONORS NEEDED"

Because the increasing number of infertile couples includes women in their thirties and forties who have little chance of getting pregnant with their own eggs or who produce no eggs at all, advertisements for egg donors appear in college newspapers or publications from infertility centers that are circulated among women in their prime childbearing years.

Most infertile couples who need egg donations have had to find their own donors. But that is not a simple matter. Couples might feel uncomfortable about making such a request of a friend or relative, or they might want to maintain their privacy. With these concerns in mind, a few medical centers in California and New York have set up egg donor programs.

For a fee, young women provide eggs for laboratory fertilization and later implantation in an infertile woman's uterus. A woman who donates eggs must have hormone injections to stimulate the ovaries to produce ripe eggs. She must also undergo blood tests, ultrasound scans, and either surgery to remove eggs or flushing to "wash out" eggs from the womb. Pay for this service is about $2,000 to $3,000. Men usually receive about $40 to $50 for sperm donations. The higher sum for egg donations reflects the added risk, time, and inconvenience for women, according to fertility experts.

Some ethicists fear that as the demand for donors goes up so will the fee. Women could then become egg vendors, not donors. Ethicists also worry that women who need the money will be exploited by more affluent couples who want and can pay for their services. College women who have donated eggs acknowledge that the fee has been a factor; they needed to pay for their education. But donors are motivated by other reasons as well.

In a report in the *New York Times*, one donor said she had fulfilled a dream to "give someone the opportunity to feel the way I did when I had a baby." Another woman, who had donated four times, said she needed the money but also felt she contributed "a terrific genetic background. All my grandparents are still living, disease-free, and they are all over 100 years old. There are no genetically transmitted diseases in my family, and all the children have high I.Q's."[4]

GENETICS OR EUGENICS?

Many people consider the idea of reproducing children with "terrific genes" as laudable and a benefit to society; they would dread passing on life-threatening or crippling genetic diseases to offspring. To reduce the risk of inherited diseases, genetic researchers have found ways to detect the presence of genes that carry disorders. Researchers have also developed tests for people who suspect or know they may pass on genetic diseases. Through testing, couples who find they are carriers may decide not to have children or may use IVF techniques to produce a healthy child.

Genetic research has also led to techniques for testing for genetic disorders in embryos and fetuses. Prenatal tests may include amniocentesis, withdrawing amniotic fluid that surrounds the fetus in the womb for biochemical analysis. Blood samples from the umbilical cord or cells that are part of the placenta may be analyzed for signs of defective genes.

Along with using biochemical tests to detect inherited diseases, researchers are using recombinant DNA techniques. (In simple terms, DNA techniques split and recombine genetic material.) These techniques help researchers examine fetal skin or blood cells and diagnose such inherited diseases as sickle cell anemia, a blood disorder, and cystic fibrosis, a lung disease. Fetal tests that show genetic disorders may lead some women to abort early in a pregnancy.

In recent years, researchers have also been able to detect abnormal genes in human sperm and eggs and to test for defects in embryos. According to the Institute of Medicine, "couples at risk for giving birth to a child with a hereditary disease could use embryo testing and in vitro fertilization as a way to have a healthy baby—a more desirable alternative to becoming pregnant, testing the fetus, and facing the prospect of having an abortion if the fetus has inherited [a] disease. Observers believe research on embryos is likely to lead to more wanted and healthy children and to a reduction in the number of abortions."[5]

While genetic manipulation can and does relieve human suffering, some bioethicists say there is a fine line between the benefits of genetic research and efforts to improve the human species through genetic breeding (in other words, attempts at eugenics). Along with NRTs, genetic manipulation is just one more scientific tool that encourages couples to try to create a "perfect product," or "perfect baby," some ethicists contend.[6]

The search for a "perfect" child raises questions about what that standard should be. Should the child be a girl or a boy? Be short or tall? Have straight or curly hair? Brown eyes or blue eyes? Big feet or little feet?

Who will decide which characteristics are "best" and which are the "least attractive"? Should scientists determine which genes are worth saving and which are not? Will government agencies require that certain types of people be produced and others not? Will genes become the criteria for determining who is qualified to populate the earth?

What will happen to people who have so-called disabilities? Who is to say what is a disability and what is not? That was part of the issue in the debate over Bree Walker's decision to bear a child with a genetic disorder (described in chapter 1). But "disorders" are not always disabilities, since many so-called disabled people lead productive, meaningful lives.

Whether or not the "perfect genes" are passed along through assisted reproduction, many infertile couples believe it is vital that one of the prospective parents provides genetic material for conception. Couples usually are convinced that by using their own genetic material they can be assured that the infant born will truly belong to them.

CONFLICTS OVER SURROGACY

The importance of the genetic connection is evident in legal transactions and controversies over whether surrogate mothers should have any custody rights to the children they bear. In a surrogate arrangement, a woman allows her womb to be used to develop an embryo, which may be created from her ovum and another's sperm or from gametes that contain none of her genetic material. In the latter situation, an embryo may be created in a laboratory and implanted later in a woman who has agreed to be a surrogate. After birth, a surrogate mother turns over the infant to the couple who has contracted for her services.

Women who offer to be childbearers for others see themselves as providing a loving, reproductive gift for relatives or friends. In the case of Ariette Schweitzer of South Dakota, it was a way to help her daughter who was born without a uterus. Schweitzer made the decision to carry the embryo conceived from her daughter's eggs and her son-in-law's sperm because she said "You do what you do for your children because you love them." In October 1991, Schweitzer gave birth to twins—her own grandchildren—saying the experience was "an honor" and that her family and friends had been support-ive throughout her pregnancy and Caesarean delivery.[7]

Paid surrogates, like paid egg donors, may also be altruistic. They are convinced they are providing a needed service for couples who cannot have children. A broker or agent, who usually receives a fee, brings together a potential surrogate and a couple who wants to have a baby.

Some paid surrogates, however, look on the entire proce-dure of carrying a baby for someone else as a business. They say they feel no emotional attachment to the child eventually born. One woman described her role as just "playing oven for a while." Another equated herself to a postal carrier, simply deliv-ering the mail.

Critics of surrogacy argue that the terms used to describe this practice disguise what is actually taking place. A woman who gives birth to a child, by virtue of the act, is the *birth* mother. But the terminology—"surrogate mother," "host womb," "gestational mother," "incubator," or whatever—effec-tively separates women from the process of childbearing.

Opponents also say that commercial surrogacy is an affront to human dignity and violates fundamental rights. They argue that paying women to have children is not only degrading but is also reminiscent of the time when children (especially girls) were routinely bought and sold or given away.

The harshest critics of paid surrogacy liken the practice to prostitution with the broker as the pimp, the one who procures a couple to pay for the use of a woman's body. Whether that analogy rings true or not, there is growing evidence that surro-gacy exploits poor and uneducated women. One surrogate broker has made it clear that he has plans to set up a business in Mexico so that he can supply U.S. clients with surrogates. The broker was confident that Mexican women would be eager to act as surrogates and would accept low fees."[8]

In the United States, women receive $10,000 and up for surrogacy arrangements, a tempting sum for anyone trying to survive on little more than that annually. The well-publicized cases of surrogates Mary Beth Whitehead, Anna Johnson, and

Elvira Jordan are examples of how women may be manipulated to "rent" their wombs. None of the women had received much more than an elementary education. They lived on low incomes and needed the funds paid for their services. The couples with whom they made surrogacy agreements were well educated and upper middle-class.

Lawsuits were brought against the women because they did not want to give up the children they bore, and publicity surrounding the cases sometimes focused on their lower-class status. The couples who could afford to pay surrogacy costs were portrayed as being better able to care for children, while the birthing mothers were considered "inadequate" because they had few material resources.

Mary Beth Whitehead's court case in 1987 was one of the first to generate public debate about the issue of surrogacy. It began two years earlier in New Jersey when Whitehead signed an agreement with William and Elizabeth Stern to be impregnated with William Stern's sperm. In other words, she would be artificially inseminated.

When Whitehead gave birth to a little girl, she said the experience of seeing and holding her baby was intensely emotional and she could not give up her child. She felt she had made a terrible mistake. Even though Whitehead at first turned over the baby to the Sterns, she later asked to have the child for a visit. She then fled to Florida with the baby, her two other children, and her husband. The FBI investigated, found the child, returned her to the Sterns, and a court case followed to determine who should have custody of "Baby M," a pseudonym that the court used in an attempt to protect the baby's privacy. After a seven-week trial, the presiding judge ruled that Mary Beth Whitehead had no parental rights to the child she had borne but that she had visitation rights.

In a 1990 California case, Anna Johnson had agreed to a surrogate arrangement with Crispina and Mark Calvert. The Calverts' embryo, created through IVF, was implanted in Johnson's uterus. After giving birth, Johnson felt the baby boy should know his birth mother and she sought visitation rights.

But the judge ruled that the Calverts were the genetic parents and that Johnson as surrogate had no parental right to the baby boy she had borne. In fact, the judge referred to Johnson as a "gestational surrogate" who merely provided a temporary home for a growing embryo/fetus.

The Elvira Jordan case, however, ended differently. In 1990 Jordan bore a child for Robert and Cynthia Moschetta. As in the Whitehead situation, Jordan is a biological as well as birth mother of a daughter. She is genetically related.

During Jordan's pregnancy, the Moschettas began divorce proceedings. In her agreement with the Moschettas, Jordan stipulated that she could not relinquish her baby if the couple divorced. The Moschettas attempted to reconcile and Jordan turned over the baby. But the Moschettas eventually divorced and in April 1991, Jordan went to court to seek custody of her child.

In her ruling, the judge noted that Cynthia Moschetta had no genetic connection to the child, thus had no legal parental rights. The judge shocked many family law and child development experts when she ruled that custody would be shared by Jordan and Robert Moschetta. Cynthia Moschetta was not allowed visitation rights.

UNANSWERED QUESTIONS ABOUT SURROGACY

Obviously, the three surrogacy cases just described, and others like them, are much more complex than the summaries indicate. They not only prompt debates about the custody of a child born to a surrogate mother, they also raise questions: Do surrogacy arrangements create a "breeder class" of women? Is commercial surrogacy a form of baby selling or is it similar to adoption arrangements in which fees are paid for services?

The answers are still being explored. Surrogacy proponents say that as long as couples want children that are genetically related to them, there will be people willing to provide that service and they should be paid. Proponents sometimes refer to surrogacy as a form of "procreative liberty" which allows women to make the decision about what they will do with their bodies.

Others contend that laws should recognize the rights of women who allow the use of their wombs to carry fetuses containing none of their genetic material. These women, according to the argument, should be seen as birth mothers, since their wombs supply needed nutrients and protection for a growing fetus. As birth mothers, they also should have a grace period, as women do in adoption arrangements, to determine whether they can relinquish the children born because of surrogacy agreements, and they should be allowed to change their minds.

Meanwhile, however, commercial surrogacy (as opposed to voluntary arrangements) has been banned in some states. Others have legalized surrogacy-for-pay, passing laws that make couples who contract for surrogacy services the legal parents of the children produced.

Perhaps one of the most wrenching questions is: How will the children of surrogate arrangements fare? Some child psychologists believe there will be traumas when young people learn they have been produced like a commodity and have been bought and sold. On the other hand, children born through surrogacy arrangements, like many adopted children, can thrive in healthy families. There is no way to be certain what the individual or social impact will be. Most children conceived under a surrogacy contract are not yet adolescents.

In spite of the many dilemmas surrounding surrogacy and the NRTs that make surrogacy possible, the basic question remains: Are women being coerced or manipulated to accept increasing medical intervention in private childbearing decisions? The question is even more pertinent in regard to medical treatment of a pregnant woman's fetus, since doctors today frequently think of and treat the fetus as a second patient, prompting more debate over a woman's role in making private decisions about her body.

Chapter
Seven

THE
"MEDICALIZATION"
OF CHILDBEARING

Before physicians acquired new medical knowledge about the fetus, and began to use new technology to treat the fetus directly, they focused on improving the overall health of the pregnant woman to ensure a healthy baby. Now, however, that focus has changed, according to some women's health advocates and civil rights groups. Because of the increased ability to treat the fetus, doctors frequently view the pregnant woman and fetus as two separate entities. As a result, the woman's needs may be ignored or given little attention, particularly if doctors (and sometimes the courts) pressure a pregnant woman to accept medical decisions that sacrifice her interests in favor of the needs of her fetus.

THE ANGELA CARDER CASE

One dramatic case of medical intervention in childbearing made news across the United States and in other parts of the world in 1987. At the time, Angela Carder was twenty-seven years old and twenty-six weeks pregnant. She was also a victim of cancer, which had abated but had suddenly reoccurred during her pregnancy. She was hospitalized at George Washington University Medical Center in Washington, D.C.

As Carder's condition deteriorated and she was close to death, her doctors advised her family that the fetus she was carrying was not developed enough to be viable, or able to live on its own. Some on the hospital staff thought Carder should undergo a cesarean section (c-section), a surgical procedure in which a physician makes an incision in a woman's abdomen and uterus to remove the baby. There was only a remote possibility that the fetus would survive the c-section and it was expected that the surgery would shorten Carder's life. Since Carder was heavily sedated, her husband and parents informed the doctor that they were convinced Carder would not want a c-section.

However, hospital administrators and legal staff apparently feared a lawsuit that would make them liable for a potentially viable fetus. Hospital lawyers, without the Carder family's knowledge, requested a ruling from a local trial court. The judge hastily convened a hearing at the hospital and interviewed Carder. Because Carder was medicated, she could not explain coherently what her decision would be about surgery; the judge concluded that she was unable to make her wishes known. He ordered the cesarean, ruling that the state had an "important and legitimate interest in protecting the potentiality of human life." He noted that because Carder was near death, he balanced this fact with the possibility of saving the fetus if delivered promptly. In his judgment, attempting to save potential life outweighed other considerations.

After the court-ordered cesarean was performed, the premature baby girl lived only two hours. Angela Carder died two days later. Her family and doctors believe her life was shortened because of the surgery.

Even though both Carder and her premature baby were dead, the American Civil Liberties Union (ACLU), on behalf of Carder's family, appealed the judge's ruling. The American Medical Association (AMA) and numerous religious and women's groups also filed legal briefs, or arguments, for the appeal. In April 1990, a Washington, D.C., court of appeals, which is equivalent to a state supreme court, overturned the trial judge's ruling and said that Carder's right to bodily integrity and her right to make an informed choice about medical treatment had been violated.

Judge John A. Terry, who wrote the majority opinion, noted:

> *To protect the right of every person to bodily integrity, courts uniformly hold that a surgeon who performs an operation without the patient's consent may be guilty of a battery.... [C]ourts do not compel one person to permit a significant intrusion upon his or her bodily integrity for the benefit of another person's health.... It has been suggested that the fetal cases are different because a [pregnant] woman...has an enhanced duty to assure the welfare of the fetus.... Surely, however, a fetus cannot have rights in this respect superior to those of a person who has already been born.*[1]

The ruling brought changes in policies at the George Washington hospital. In November 1990, the hospital stated in an agreement filed with the court that it would "respect patient autonomy" and "whenever possible" would accept patients' decisions on their treatment even if those decisions did not conform to medical recommendations.[2]

Besides the Angela Carder case, there have been at least a dozen other court-ordered cesareans in the United States. In addition, pregnant women have been detained in the hospital against their wishes so that doctors could monitor the welfare of their fetuses. Women have also been forced to accept blood transfusions even though their religious beliefs prohibited receiving blood.

WHO DETERMINES PREGNANT WOMEN'S MEDICAL CARE?

For years, medical and legal experts have been debating whether or not pregnant women are being pressured to accept the medical technology available to treat a fetus. Physicians may require pregnant women to undergo such procedures as ultrasound scanning (X rays to observe the fetus); amniocentesis (a needle is inserted into the womb to test the fluid surrounding the fetus and determine whether there are abnormalities); and "fetal therapy," which may involve surgery or other medical treatment on the fetus in the womb.

Some pregnant women accept such procedures as a welcome part of their prenatal care. Others, however, fear the possible risks of such techniques, or they may object to the kind of "high-tech" control over their childbearing. Many women insist they should be provided with information about prenatal health care, but should then be allowed to make their own decisions about their treatment during pregnancy.

A 1987 survey at the University of Illinois found that 46 percent of the directors of maternal-fetal research programs thought that pregnant women who refused medical advice, thereby endangering their fetuses, should be held legally liable.[3] The researchers' views reflect those of some legal experts who have argued that there are limits to a woman's freedom when she conceives and chooses to carry a fetus to term.

University of Texas law professor John Robertson has been one of the most vigorous advocates of what he and others call the "duty of care." In Robertson's view, women should have a legal responsibility to ensure that a healthy baby is born; any negligent acts that would harm or injure a fetus should be considered fetal abuse. His basic argument is that a pregnant woman who carries to term is obligated to protect her fetus. He believes those obligations may require her to avoid work, recreation, and medical care choices that are hazardous to the fetus. They also obligate her to preserve her health for the fetus' sake or even allow established therapies to be performed on an affected fetus. Finally, they require that she undergo prenatal screening when there is reason to believe that this screening may identify congenital defects correctable with available therapies.[4]

While most people would agree that it is reasonable to expect pregnant women to follow health care practices that do not endanger their fetuses, the idea that women should be legally obligated to provide that care poses many other questions. How, for example, can pregnant women obtain "proper" health care if it is not available or is not affordable? Who should make the decision about what is obligatory health care? Should medical professionals also play the role of lawyer and judge? What about the right of a competent person to refuse medical treatment? Is a pregnant woman somehow "incompetent" if she does not accept the recommendations of a physician or judge or whoever else imposes decisions on her?

In an article for the *Journal of the American Medical Association*, two bioethicists, Lawrence J. Nelson and Nancy Milliken, contend that a pregnant woman is ethically obligated to care for her fetus, but she should not be legally forced to do so. Court-ordered treatment, in their view,

> *invades a woman's privacy, entails the disclosure of confidential medical and personal information, and thrusts the woman into the adversarial system, where she must defend her choices on a highly personal matter when she is…ill-disposed to do so. Moreover, the request for a court order demonstrates the physician's willingness to use physical force against a competent adult to effect treatment, an ethically perilous course of action for a physician to adopt under any circumstances.*[5]

Other experts say that lawyers and judges see themselves as advocates for the fetus, so they bring lawsuits on the basis of medical judgments rather than legal precedents. According to biologist Ruth Hubbard, it is "warped logic" to allow medical opinions to have the force of law. She asks: Is a judge a more appropriate person to decide the fate of a fetus "than the woman whose body sustains the fetus and who will be physically, emotionally, and economically affected by whatever is done?"[6]

Even when a woman maintains good health all through her pregnancy, she may have little choice in how or where she gives birth. Because of the so-called medicalization of childbearing and public concerns about protecting women during childbirth, the majority of pregnant women give birth in hospitals. Yet a ten-year study of childbearing worldwide, conducted by a team of forty researchers at Oxford University in England and led by Murray Enkin, a professor of obstetrics at McMaster University in Canada, shows that although many hospitals provide excellent obstetric care, up to sixty hospital procedures provide little benefit and may even be dangerous to mothers and their babies.

One example is the birthing position required in many hospitals. A woman usually must lie on her back, with the pelvis tilted and feet in stirrups. Researchers found that such a position "can adversely affect labor by interfering with the blood supply of mother and baby," according to a report in *Parade Magazine*. The magazine also reported that "When the mother is *allowed* to select positions during labor, she is likely to choose standing or walking for the first stages. She will feel less pain and need less pain medication if the birth canal is open wide. If she needs to lie down, she will elect to lie on her side during delivery, or she may squat and deliver the baby with her own hands."[7]

The Oxford study, which is available as a computer database and in book form (*A Guide to Effective Care in Pregnancy and Childbirth*) from Oxford University Press, also criticized the common practice of isolating healthy newborns in nurseries as a way to prevent infections from the mother. The study found that infections often spread to healthy babies in nurseries, and that it was safer for newborns to stay in the same room with their mothers, who have carried them and have probably immunized them.

Some women have been actively engaged in efforts to give women more choices in childbearing and have been encouraging midwifery, or the use of midwife services. Midwives commonly assisted in childbearing prior to the mid-1900s. At that time, midwives usually had no formal medical education but had experience in helping relatives and friends with childbirth. They attended nearly half of the U.S. births until the past few decades. By 1972, the medical profession had taken control of nearly all birthing procedures, and doctors attended 99 percent of births.[8]

Because women once more are turning to midwifery for assistance in childbearing, teaching hospitals in metropolitan areas such as Boston, Philadelphia, Cleveland, and Chicago are offering masters' and doctors' degrees in nurse-midwifery. The nurse-midwife is a registered nurse and usually attends births in special hospital birth centers. In some states, however, they provide home services for people in isolated rural areas or in urban areas where pregnant women of some ethnic groups have always been attended by midwives. The traditional type of midwife (trained through apprenticeship and experience) also attends some home births.

Women choose midwifery for a number of reasons. They may want more say over the birth process itself. As long as a woman's pregnancy is normal, she may prefer to give birth in the comfort and security of her own home rather than in a hospital setting where she will be required to conform to a set routine for birthing procedures. A midwife can spend more time with a woman during her prenatal visits than a doctor can, and may show more respect for a pregnant woman's feelings and opinions.

A midwife can also be present during most of the labor. (States that licence nurse-midwives usually require that a doctor be available during childbirth but not necessarily in the delivery room.) In the opinion of one Chicago-area mother, a midwife is "more like a supportive friend" who allows a woman some control and choices during her pregnancy and in the birth process.[9]

The matter of choice is also an issue in whether a woman gives birth vaginally or by cesarean section (c-section). In a vaginal birth, a woman experiences labor, or involuntary contractions that force a baby through the birth canal until it is born. But doctors may intervene in the birth process and order delivery by c-section. Usually doctors perform cesareans when they perceive danger to the fetus or mother in a vaginal birth. The baby's head may be too large for the pelvic opening, for example.

Cesarean section has helped decrease maternal and infant death over the years. But the number of c-sections performed has been increasing rapidly; one in four women today have surgical births. The national rate of c-sections rose from 5.5 percent of all deliveries in 1970 to 24 percent of all deliveries by 1986, with an expected increase to 40 percent by the year 2000. For many women the surgery is unnecessary, according to Dr. Sidney M. Wolfe, who directs the Public Citizen Health Research Group, a patient advocacy group founded by Ralph Nader. Wolfe pointed out in his book, *Women's Health Alert: What Most Doctors Won't Tell You About*, that numerous surveys of hospitals in the United States show that public hospitals have the lowest rate of c-sections, while private for-profit hospitals perform the most c-sections.[10]

Many cesareans are performed on women who had surgical deliveries for previous pregnancies, even though the long-held theory that women who had once had a cesarean could not safely give birth vaginally has been disproved. Now obstetricians and gynecologists recommend that women who previously had cesarean deliveries try vaginal births. Yet a study conducted by Randall Stafford of the University of California at Berkeley found that a woman was more likely to repeat a cesarean if she had health insurance and went to a private hospital. Surgical births cost at least $2,000 more than vaginal deliveries, so a hospital can realize higher profits from cesarean deliveries. Certainly most doctors who order cesarean sections believe they are the safest and best procedure for the pregnant women they are treating. But Stafford's study concluded that profit motives can affect whether or not doctors will recommend surgical procedures for a birth.[11]

Chapter
Eight

PROTECTING
OR POLICING
MOTHERS-TO-BE?

With the increasing medical attention given to the fetus and the widespread availability of information on fetal health hazards, many individuals and groups have set themselves up as watchdogs of pregnant women. Once a woman is visibly pregnant she may be considered public property, and people feel free to tell her what to do and how to behave:

"You shouldn't be drinking that champagne," a guest advised a pregnant woman who was hostessing a party celebrating her husband's birthday.

"You should sit in the nonsmoking section," a waiter scolded a soon-to-be-mother whom he seated with smoking friends in a restaurant.

"You don't want that job—you might be exposed to toxic substances that will harm your baby!" a supervisor in a manufacturing plant lectured a pregnant worker.

"You ought to be home on a day like this! You might fall on the ice!" a driver yelled at a pregnant woman walking across a parking lot on a cold, snowy day.

BUSYBODIES OR CITIZEN PROTECTORS?

When people feel duty-bound to warn a pregnant woman of hazards or to harangue her if she doesn't behave as told, her

69

privacy can be easily invaded. An incident that occurred in Seattle, Washington, is a case in point. A pregnant woman (who would not allow her name to be used in news reports) went to a Seattle restaurant to have dinner with a friend and ordered a strawberry daiquiri before the meal. A waiter informed the customer that alcohol could harm her fetus. When the pregnant customer said she wanted the cocktail, the waiter discussed the matter with a co-worker, who peeled a warning label from a beer bottle and took it to the customer's table. A federal law requires that beer containers include the cautionary statement "drinking during pregnancy can cause birth defects." Some states also require that the warning signs be posted in places where liquor is served.

The Seattle woman said she had read a great deal about the effects of alcohol on a fetus and "had been very careful" throughout her pregnancy. She had just seen her doctor because she was due to give birth at any time; she thought it would be safe to have the drink she had ordered with dinner. "I went there to eat, not to drink," she said, adding that the two restaurant servers "were just plain rude" and treated her like a child abuser. She was so upset that she complained to an assistant manager, who fired both workers. A week after the incident, the woman gave birth to a healthy boy.

Meanwhile, the two fired restaurant workers began a campaign to establish state regulations about serving alcoholic beverages to pregnant women. Some Washington state legislators and news media commentators believe laws should restrict alcohol use by pregnant women, even though medical experts generally agree that a few drinks during a pregnancy probably will not harm the fetus. The American College of Obstetricians and Gynecologists warn, however, that a woman who has several drinks per day could give birth to a child with fetal alcohol syndrome, a condition related to mental retardation, slow physical growth, and other defects.

If rules are adopted to prevent women from consuming alcoholic beverages, civil libertarians say that the regulations would be violating a woman's right to privacy and her right to make her own choices. "It becomes a slippery slope when you talk about somebody else [beside the pregnant woman] making that decision.... Any form of government has to stay out of women's reproductive rights and individual lives and bodies," a lawyer with the Woman's Law Center in Seattle said.[1]

Some legal experts and public health officials believe the widespread scrutiny of pregnant women has already entered the slippery slope. In other words, legal actions will not stop at a certain point but will slide to a destructive end. If pregnant women are policed and prosecuted because their behavior *might* harm a fetus, then they are criminal suspects from the moment they conceive.

In the opinion of Katha Pollitt, who writes extensively on women's issues, the current emphasis on the health and rights of the fetus

> *posits a world in which women will be held accountable, on sketchy or no evidence, for birth defects; in which all fertile women will be treated as potentially pregnant all the time; in which courts, employers, social workers and doctors—not to mention nosy neighbors and vengeful male partners—will monitor women's behavior.*[2]

If pregnant women were constantly monitored for possible hazards to the fetus, any number of different types of behavior, from changing the cat litter to strenuous exercise, would be suspect. That, in the view of some observers, turns pregnancy into imprisonment.

"PREGNANCY POLICE"

The increased emphasis nationwide on possible hazards to the fetus has prompted not only more scrutiny of pregnant women in everyday situations, but more aggressive policing of pregnant women suspected of drug use. In 1986, police officers in San Diego, California, arrested Pamela Rae Stewart, an occasional drug user, because she did not follow her doctor's advice and her infant son died soon after birth. Stewart had a condition known as placenta abruptio, in which the placenta may pull away from the uterus. Her doctor had advised her not to have intercourse and to go to the hospital immediately if she began to bleed.

When Stewart began bleeding, she disregarded her doctor's advice and waited about twelve hours before going to the hospital. Stewart's baby was born with massive brain damage and died soon after birth. An examining doctor found traces of amphetamines in the infant's blood, but concluded that excessive hemorrhaging was the cause of the child's death.

Yet a hospital official called the child protective agency, who then called the police. The police informed the district attorney's office, and the prosecutor ordered Stewart's arrest, charging her under the California Penal Code for "willful failure to provide medical attention to a minor child." Eventually, the case was thrown out of court, because the law under which Stewart was charged did not apply to her situation.[3]

Stewart's case was one of several in recent years that have come about in part because of public outrage over the many babies born damaged in utero by drugs, including alcohol and tobacco, that their mothers have used. A national survey of 36 hospitals in 1988 found that about 11 percent of all newborns, or about 375,000 infants, were exposed to illegal drugs while in the womb. The images of such infants have appeared on TV screens or in newspapers and magazines, and they are hard to forget: tiny forms hooked to tubes and oxygen masks, barely alive and suffering withdrawal symptoms from prenatal drug abuse. Some of the babies are born infected with HIV because their parents are intravenous (IV) drug users. (IV drug users share contaminated needles and spread the infection that leads to AIDS.)

In many cases, the drug-damaged babies require intensive and long-term care that has cost the nation hundreds of millions of dollars. During one year in Los Angeles County alone, extended hospital stays for drug-exposed newborns cost $32 million. Public funds paid for most expenses, or the hospital absorbed the costs.

There are additional public costs when drug-exposed babies are abandoned in hospitals or are placed in foster care. Public schools must also spend much more to educate children who suffer health or learning problems caused by prenatal drug abuse. In Los Angeles, the annual amount is about $15,000 per child, more than three times that of the cost for educating a child in a regular classroom.[4]

Many legal experts and social service professionals believe that women who give birth to drug-damaged children should be dealt with in family or juvenile courts, which try to find treatment for people with serious problems rather than issue punishments. These courts attempt to provide needed services such as placing children in foster care if required, and getting treatment for an addicted mother.

But a large number of Americans believe pregnant women should be criminally punished if they abuse drugs and cause fetal damage. The *Atlanta Constitution* conducted one survey of 1,500 people in a fifteen-state area and found that 71 percent of the respondents favored criminal prosecution for women whose illegal drug use during pregnancy had harmed their infants.

Since 1987, prosecutors in at least nineteen states have brought criminal charges in sixty to eighty cases against pregnant drug addicts; in 1989, the state of Florida was the first to convict a cocaine addict of delivering drugs to her fetus.[5] Prosecutors emphasize that addicts are engaging in unlawful acts that should not be condoned. But they say the purpose behind nearly all of the cases in which pregnant addicts have been criminally charged is to get women into a treatment program so that children can be protected. They believe that the threat of a jail sentence is the most effective way to force treatment.

DISPUTES OVER TREATMENT OF PREGNANT ADDICTS

In several highly publicized instances, however, criminal charges brought against pregnant addicts have created widespread controversy. Consider the case of Lynn Bremmer, a lawyer in Muskegon, Michigan, who was addicted to cocaine. During her pregnancy in 1990, Bremmer discussed her addiction with her doctor and admitted using cocaine about forty hours before she gave birth. When tests revealed traces of the drug in her baby's urine, the county prosecutor brought felony charges, accusing Bremmer of passing cocaine to her newborn baby through her umbilical cord. He avoided a charge of delivering drugs to a fetus, which would have raised many arguments about "fetal personhood."

Several months earlier, another Muskegon woman, Kimberly Hardy, had been arrested on a similar charge. Both Hardy and Bremmer lost custody of their children and were required to enter drug treatment programs. They also faced charges of child neglect.

In February 1991, a circuit court judge dismissed the charges against Bremmer, saying that the law was misapplied. The judge said the Michigan statute prohibiting the distribution of illegal drugs was not intended to apply to cases like Bremmer's. According to the judge, the felony charges against Bremmer violated her right to privacy "by intruding into her relationship with her fetus without a compelling reason to do so," and denied her constitutional right to equal protection under the law—she had not been informed that the law would apply to her.

What about Kimberly Hardy? The Michigan Court of Appeals ruled in April 1991 that she would not be tried for child abuse. Both Hardy and Bremmer completed drug treatment programs and have regained custody of their children.[6]

In spite of the apparent success of forced drug treatment in the two Michigan cases, and a few others that have been reported nationwide, many health workers and civil libertarians criticize state prosecutors who aggressively pursue pregnant addicts. Critics say authorities target primarily the poor and people of color. Over the past few years, at least 80 percent of the women who have been prosecuted have been black, Hispanic, Asian, or members of other minority groups, according to statistics compiled by the American Civil Liberties Union.

Yet drug use and abuse is prevalent across all segments of society. In fact, research indicates that 15 percent of all pregnant women use drugs. Middle-class and affluent women are more likely to use marijuana while poor women are apt to use cocaine. That may be one reason there is unequal treatment of pregnant addicts. Marijuana is perceived as being less harmful to the fetus than cocaine, say researchers at the National Center for Perinatal Addiction Research and Education in Chicago. There are also indications that public health facilities, where most poor women receive obstetric services, may be more aggressive in reporting and prosecuting pregnant addicts.[7]

Those who oppose criminalizing addiction point out that substance abuse and alcoholism are diseases, which they believe should be approached as public health problems, not as criminal acts. Since some states require medical personnel to report drug addiction among pregnant women, many of the women avoid prenatal care and drug treatment because they fear betrayal and arrest.

If health officials are summoned to appear in court, they may have to reveal confidences and verify that pregnant women have come to them because of drug abuse. Prosecutors use such testimony to help bring about criminal convictions for pregnant addicts. Some health officials say a better way to deal with the problem is to improve education, medical care, and drug treatment facilities.

THE NEED FOR PRENATAL CARE

Opponents of the punitive approach to addiction emphasize the fact that low-income pregnant women are seldom able to get into drug treatment centers. Private facilities may exclude patients who depend on federal- or state-funded medical programs to pay for services. Regardless of whether patients can pay for care, private centers usually refuse to take pregnant women because they do not have obstetrical staff or other needed services.

Public facilities may also be unable to offer the kind of

prenatal care, social services, economic help, and child care that pregnant addicts need. The lack of child care is one of the major barriers to treatment. A pregnant addict with children at home is usually not allowed to take her children with her to a day-treatment center or a residential facility. So unless a partner or relative is able to care for her children, the addict cannot enter a treatment program.

Poor education and lack of transportation are other major barriers. Even if pregnant addicts are able to receive treatment, they may not be able to continue with recovery unless they can read the guidance materials and attend follow-up therapy sessions.

Some observers believe there is also a lack of national political will to provide women with the kind of prenatal care that could help prevent addiction. Only a small number of states—Washington, Oregon, Wisconsin, Rhode Island, Maryland, and Virginia among them—have begun to provide more comprehensive treatment programs, which include help with detoxification, child care, housing, and education.

Rather than prosecuting pregnant addicts, Americans need to make a greater commitment to establishing treatment and prevention programs, according to James E. Long, director of the Illinois Department of Alcoholism and Substance Abuse. Long is convinced that such programs work. He noted that in 1990, forty-seven out of fifty pregnant addicts who entered a state-funded program in Chicago were able to give birth to healthy, drug-free infants.[8]

Women who are not drug abusers also face major obstacles to prenatal care. Women make up the second largest group of poor in the nation (children are the largest group in poverty), and poor women can seldom afford to pay medical expenses. In addition, poor pregnant women may suffer from a variety of health problems that affect the children they bear. They are likely to produce premature, low birthweight babies, who are liable to such side effects as seizures, respiratory tract problems, poor vision, and other physical defects.

In recent years, cuts in federal and state funds have forced many public health clinics to reduce nutritional services and medical care for poor expectant women. Some women have to wait from several weeks to several months for their first prenatal visit to a clinic. The problem is compounded by the fact that in some parts of the nation, particularly rural and inner city areas, the number of doctors who provide maternity services has decreased. Even when maternity services are available, doctors may not accept patients who are uninsured or who depend on government payments of fees. Frequently, government payments are much less than a doctor's usual charges and require extensive paperwork to collect.

Lack of adequate insurance coverage is another major barrier to maternity care (as well as other types of health care). As many political leaders and health officials have noted, an estimated 37 million Americans are without medical insurance. The situation is quite different in other industrialized nations such as Canada, Sweden, France, and Germany, where national health insurance programs help pay medical expenses for all citizens, regardless of income.

Because of the barriers to prenatal care and cuts in federal programs that provide health care, the U.S. infant mortality rate is higher than that of nineteen other industrialized nations. From about 1965 to the mid-1980s, infant deaths in the United States declined, but since the 1980s progress has faltered. Today the infant mortality rate is just over 10 per 1,000 live births. In some areas of the United States, though, the infant mortality rate ranges from 15 to over 20 deaths per 1,000 live births.[9]

The Children's Defense Fund (CDF) and other groups working to improve the lives of children say that a nationwide approach is needed to get adequate health care to pregnant women. Adequate prenatal care is one of the best ways to improve infants' health and reduce infant deaths, CDF says. The organization calls for an investment of more funds in programs such as the supplemental food program (known as WIC) for women, infants, and children. Community and Migrant Health Centers and Maternal and Child Health

Block Grants are other successful programs; they bring health services to communities that have little or no such care.

WHAT ABOUT THE FATHERS?

While a great deal of public attention has been focused on the behavior of pregnant women, many women's rights advocates wonder when equal attention will be given to the behavior of fathers. "When will men be held accountable?" they ask. "Why should only women be responsible for producing healthy babies?"

Some commentators note that there is little public outrage over men who abandon pregnant partners, leaving them without emotional support and contributing little or nothing to the cost of caring for children they helped conceive. As a result, the number of women—especially single mothers—and children in poverty has been increasing steadily, which means more women and children will face health risks.

Women's rights advocates pose another question: What about men who abuse pregnant women? Family violence experts estimate that one in every twelve pregnant women suffers a severe beating from her partner at least once while she is carrying a fetus. Beatings can cause a woman to miscarry or give birth to an injured or dead baby.

Men may also be responsible for other kinds of injuries to the unborn. In recent years, studies have shown that smoking, drug abuse, and exposure to nuclear radiation and toxic substances are linked to the production of defective sperm, perhaps causing injury to a fetus. No one is sure whether dangerous materials affect the sperm by altering genes or are passed on to the woman, damaging the egg. But scientists believe that whatever flaws are produced, they occur at the time of conception.

In one study, British researchers found that children of male workers at a nuclear power plant had a higher incidence of leukemia than children whose fathers worked elsewhere. Another study, published in the *American Journal of Public*

Health in 1990, indicated that babies of Vietnam War veterans suffered more birth defects than children of other veterans. The Vietnam veterans were exposed to a weed killer that contained dioxin, a highly toxic chemical linked to cancer and other serious diseases. Studies also show that men who drink alcohol or smoke heavily may be responsible for offspring with low birthweight and various birth defects, including disorders of the central nervous system. And the American Association for the Advancement of Science reported in 1991 that fathers exposed to toxic materials on their jobs may be just as likely to cause damage to their children as mothers who are exposed to toxins.[10]

Research on how exposure to damaging substances can affect men and their offspring has been sparse. But studies are increasing, primarily because of debates about employer policies that have barred women from jobs that could pose a danger to a fetus. These jobs could also be hazardous to men and their reproductive functions.

Chapter
Nine

PREGNANCY
AND WORKPLACE
ISSUES

Although federal laws forbid discrimination against pregnant women in the workplace, many working women and women who apply for jobs have faced discriminatory practices. Some have been forced to leave a job or have been barred from jobs that supposedly can endanger a fetus.

During the early 1900s, when many workplaces were extremely hazardous, laws were passed to protect the safety and health of workers. But some of those laws were designed to provide more protective measures for women than for men, since women were considered "unfit" or "too fragile" or "too emotional" for many occupations, or were thought to be immoral if they mingled with men in the workplace.

In a 1909 case (*Muller v. Oregon*), a worker challenged an Oregon state law that limited women to a ten-hour workday but allowed men to work without restrictions. (At the time, people usually worked from sunup to sundown—twelve- to fourteen-hour workdays were common.) The U.S. Supreme Court upheld the law, ruling that the government had an obligation to assure that mothers would be healthy and would produce healthy children. Limiting the workdays of men would be an infringement of their rights and would be unreasonable because women were dependent on men for survival.

A number of other state laws have prohibited women from

working in occupations such as bartending and construction, professions like law and medicine, and even from serving on juries. When these laws were challenged, the justices frequently reasoned that it was improper for women to be involved in rough-and-tumble worldly affairs. Because of their supposedly "delicate nature," women needed extra protection—not equal protection as provided in the Fourteenth Amendment to the Constitution.

The Civil Rights Act of 1964 helped change some discriminatory practices in the workplace. A section of the law, called Title VII, prohibits job discrimination on the basis of race, national origin, religion, and gender. In 1978, Congress passed the Pregnancy Discrimination Act (PDA), which amended Title VII. The PDA stipulates that a pregnant worker (or a worker who may become pregnant) must be treated like others on a particular job unless she is unable to do the work. Yet a number of discriminatory practices against pregnant women have continued, both when pregnant women apply for jobs and when they are on the job.

EMPLOYMENT PRACTICES AFFECTING PREGNANT WOMEN

When applying for a job, should a pregnant woman reveal her status? This question was one topic of discussion at a recent Chicago conference on business ethics that explored issues employers and employees face with the influx of women in the workforce. Conference participants noted that the question of revealing a pregnancy would not have been discussed thirty or forty years ago because men dominated the labor force.

Some participants said they believe women should be truthful about their pregnancies because employers have the right to know about situations that might affect their business. But others disagreed, noting that employers may consider the pregnancy a liability and therefore refuse to hire or promote a woman.

If the job makes a difference in whether or not a woman feeds her family, then concealing a pregnancy is an ethical approach, in the view of Sharon Kinsella, director of Nine to

Five, a national women's organization dealing with employment problems. Kinsella added that a pregnancy is "nobody's business" except the pregnant woman's and whoever helped her conceive.[1]

Pregnant women may also be forced to resign from a job before it is necessary to do so. For example, in 1985 when Geralyn Montoya, head cashier at a supermarket in Las Vegas, New Mexico, told her manager she was pregnant, he required her to begin training a replacement for her job. The manager also cut Montoya's work hours and changed her duties. She was denied a pregnancy leave and was not permitted to return to her job after her baby was born. She charged the supermarket with discrimination in a lawsuit (*Montoya v. Super Save Warehouse Foods*), and in 1991 a jury awarded her $50,000 in compensation.[2]

Telephone workers at Western Electric (now part of AT&T) filed a similar lawsuit in the late 1970s after they were required to resign from their jobs because of pregnancy. They won a settlement of $66 million, which was distributed among 13,000 women.

During recent years, "fetal protection" policies have barred women from jobs considered hazardous to fetal health. The policies required women to perform other less-hazardous work or be sterilized in order to keep jobs that might expose them to toxins that could be passed on to a fetus. Companies said they adopted the policies as a safety measure for employees, although the health of fetuses seemed to be the uppermost concern. The policies were, in part, a way for firms to guard against liability suits from employees' children who might be born with disabilities due to exposure to toxins. But in 1991, the Supreme Court declared that fetal protection policies violated the Civil Rights Act and the PDA amendment.

THE JOHNSON CONTROLS CASE

The High Court decision on fetal protection policies was the result of a lawsuit brought against Johnson Controls, a battery manufacturer that has plants across the nation. In 1982, the company established a protective policy that barred women of childbearing age from jobs where high levels of lead were present. One type of job which required heating lead to form posts for batteries paid better than average wages because of the risk of exposure to fumes.

Lead is extremely toxic, and if inhaled or ingested can cause serious health problems, such as disorders of the nervous system or damage to the reproductive systems of both men and women. If lead moves into a pregnant woman's bloodstream it can pass through the umbilical cord to the fetus, causing learning disabilities or nerve damage.

In some cases, lead levels can be reduced if a person leaves the source of exposure for an extensive period of time. At Johnson Controls, workers with high lead levels in their blood transferred to cleaner but lower-paying jobs until their lead concentrations decreased. But the company's protective policy changed this practice for women. A woman could stay at the job only if she could prove that she had been sterilized or was unable to conceive.

Some workers angrily protested through their union, the United Automobile Workers. But because they needed the income, several women had themselves sterilized in order to keep working at the higher-risk jobs, or they transferred to lower-paying jobs. The United Automobile Workers eventually sued Johnson Controls. But a federal district court dismissed the case, saying the company had a legitimate business interest in setting the protective policy in order to avoid lawsuits from employees' offspring. The union appealed, first to the U.S. circuit court which upheld the dismissal, and then to the U.S. Supreme Court.

After the High Court heard the case (*Automobile Workers v. Johnson Controls*), all nine justices agreed that the lower court had acted improperly and that Johnson Controls had violated Title VII of the Civil Rights Act, although several justices said that some type of fetal protection policies might be acceptable under the law. In the majority opinion, written by Justice Harry Blackmun, the Court found "obvious" bias in Johnson Controls' policy. "Fertile men, but not fertile women, are given a choice as to whether they wish to risk their reproductive health for a particular job," Blackmun wrote.

The justices cited evidence, which the lower courts had ignored, that men as well as women could suffer damage to their reproductive systems from lead poisoning. They also noted that eight women employed at Johnson Controls had become pregnant while their blood lead levels were high, but none of their babies were injured. The Court concluded that "Decisions about the welfare of future children must be left to the parents who conceive, bear, support and raise them rather than to the employers who hire those parents."[3]

Because of the ruling, other major corporations, including a number of chemical and petroleum companies, had to rescind protective policies they had established. Some business officials said that without the policies companies would be open to all kinds of liability suits; some might stop operations in order to avoid risks to the unborn.

Yet companies can avoid liability by following the safety guidelines of state work safety laws and the U.S. Occupational Safety and Health Administration regulations. Companies can also avoid lawsuits by informing employees of any known risks in doing their jobs.

Some legal and medical experts emphasize that if companies are concerned about risks to female employees who might become pregnant they should try to eliminate those risks for males, too, since studies are beginning to show that a variety of workplace hazards can affect the male reproductive system. Researchers at the University of North Carolina, for example, studied data on 4,000 fathers and their children and found that infants of men working in textile industries and mining, and artists exposed to some toxic paints, had a higher-than-average risk of premature births, low birthweights, or stillbirths. Aircraft workers and car mechanics were at above-average risk of fathering children with leukemia.[4]

Women's rights advocates were extremely pleased with the Supreme Court decision on fetal protection policies, because it made a statement about the right of women to control their own bodies. In addition, the decision halted efforts to establish protective policies that could bar women from many other jobs.

Chapter
Ten

GLOBAL
REPRODUCTIVE
CONCERNS

The United States is not the only country struggling with reproductive issues. Most industrialized countries are calling for responsible and ethical use of the new reproductive technologies, presenting arguments similar to those that Americans express. National policies on abortion are also debated. But in many less affluent countries, a major issue is population growth.

Most industrialized countries have stabilized their populations, but in poor, developing nations, populations are exploding. Poor people may have many children in order to assure family survival—children help out with farm labor, food gathering, or other work to provide basic needs. Or those in poverty may have little choice in whether or not they procreate, since they seldom have access to birth control measures. Customs may also prevent use of birth control devices.

As populations grow, they create demands on limited local resources, which in turn leads to serious economic and social problems. Yet poor nations are not consuming as much of the world's resources as rich countries. The industrialized nations make up only 20 percent of the world's population, but consume 80 percent of the earth's resources. As less affluent nations strive to improve their economies and ways of life, they also want to make use of lumber, water supplies, farmland, and other resources; this sometimes pits one group or nation against another. Rapid population growth makes competition even worse and is one of the major barriers to economic development.

RAPID POPULATION GROWTH

For the first three to five million years of human history, world population was fairly stable, with the birth rate and death rate almost equal and both quite high. In other words, there was zero population growth; people replaced themselves but did not add to the total number of humans on earth.

Then as people became better fed, learned to overcome diseases, and lived longer, the death rate fell and the birth rate rose. In some parts of the world, people began to limit the number of births and were able to maintain a stable population, but this has not been the case everywhere. In parts of Asia and Africa, for example, populations have grown dramatically.

In the 1800s, the world population stood at one billion. It had increased to two billion by 1930, and by 1960 had soared rapidly to three billion. Fifteen years later, another billion was added. By 1987, more than five billion people were on earth, and by 2000, the world population will be more than six billion. Another billion will be added in the decade or so after that.[1]

Billions and millions are difficult to comprehend. But those statistics can be broken down to twenty-four new people added to the world's population every six seconds—the time it took to read this sentence. Within an hour, the world's population increases by 11,000 people; by the end of a day 260,000 newborns arrive on the planet.[2]

In many societies, bearing and rearing children become heavy burdens for women who must also spend long hours each day at hard labor growing or gathering food and preparing meals. Most women in poor nations have many children spaced close together, which not only endangers their lives but the health of their children as well. Each day an estimated 42,000 infants die before they reach their first birthdays, primarily because of premature births (often due to poor or no prenatal care for mothers), malnutrition and starvation, and lack of health care.

Poor women seldom receive a formal education and have little or no access to information about family planning or contraceptive methods. Studies have shown a direct link between educational level and birth rates. In countries that promote literacy and educational achievement among women, birth rates drop. Educated women usually marry later and make use of family planning information; they use contraceptives more often and have fewer children than women with no schooling.

FAMILY PLANNING

Almost every country in the world has some type of family planning policy. The approach each nation takes to family planning depends on its economic status, cultural patterns, religious beliefs, political climate, and how much authority the government has over citizens' lives. In some countries, governments and political groups may inhibit or prevent family planning efforts. But in others, legislators may pass laws that provide for programs to carry out family planning.

Private groups may also be involved. For example, women's organizations, industries, and schools may provide information about birth control. Nonprofit groups and companies that develop and sell contraceptive devices may support family planning services as well.

Family planning services may include prenatal health care along with birth control information and distribution of contraceptives. Some governments offer incentives—cash or gifts to women who make use of birth control devices; abortion may also be an option for limiting the size of families.

Even when family planning programs are available, many women are barred from birth control information and contraceptive use because of male attitudes. By custom African women, for example, marry young, have low status, and are forced to be subservient to men; they are unable to exert enough influence to demand wide use of contraceptives. In most African countries, women are only able to limit the number of children they bear (the average is six or seven) by breastfeeding their babies for up to two or three years, which suppresses the ovulation cycle, or by long periods of sexual abstinence.

In Pakistan, which has the highest population growth in southern Asia, the average woman also has six or seven children. The government has attempted to provide birth control resources because the country's population is expected to soar from 110 million to more than 300 million by 2020. The nation's largest city will increase from over 6 million to 30 million. But Islamic religious leaders and many older Pakistani men oppose birth control because they believe "more population means more manpower," which in turn will strengthen the Islamic faith in the nation. Yet the country faces food shortages, massive health and social problems from overcrowding, and increases in illiteracy because of uncontrolled population growth, say Pakistani health workers.[3]

Latin American countries also have extremely high birth rates. Since the Catholic Church, which is opposed to birth control, has a strong influence in Latin America, few public or private agencies provide family planning. Brazil, the world's largest Roman Catholic country, did not legalize birth control until 1988; people generally have little information about or access to contraceptives. Birth control devices are available in drug stores, but not in state health clinics where poor women are likely to go for care. Nevertheless, Brazilian women do find ways to control pregnancies.

Brazilian laws prohibit sterilization and abortion unless a woman's life is in danger. But both procedures are common forms of birth control. A recent Associated Press report noted that "28 percent of Brazilian women of childbearing age have been sterilized," a rate that far exceeds countries like France where 5 percent of the women are sterilized.

Poor women frequently are sterilized by having their fallopian tubes tied during cesarean sections. Doctors order the cesareans saying the surgical deliveries are needed to protect women's health. However, the federal health service pays for the surgery, and poor women choose the surgical delivery and sterilization because they cannot afford contraceptives and the costs of rearing large families.[4]

APPROACHES TO ABORTION

Around the world poor women, who sometimes regret the children they bear because they do not have the resources to care for them, may use whatever measures are available to limit pregnancies. Women in many nations with prohibitions against abortion except as a life-saving measure still opt to end a pregnancy, legally or not, as a means of birth control. Frequently women choose dangerous, unsanitary practices to abort; the consequences are tragic deaths.

One international study showed that when Romania's dictator banned abortion and contraception in 1966 in order to increase birth rates, mortality rates among women aged fifteen to forty-four increased sevenfold over the next twelve years. In addition, because women were forced to have children they could not afford, thousands of Romanian babies were abandoned or placed for adoption. On the other hand, Czechoslovakia liberalized its abortion laws, and abortion-related deaths dropped 56 percent during one four-year period and 38 percent during another four-year stretch.[5]

On a global scale, between at least 100,000 and 200,000 women die each year because of botched illegal abortions. In poor countries where abortion-related deaths are high and birth control methods are not widely used or are prohibited, national leaders are faced with difficult ethical questions. For example, is it ethical or moral to risk the lives and health of women and the children already born in order to maintain religious, cultural, and patriarchal views on reproductive matters? If a nation is overpopulated, is it the government's responsibility to control reproduction in order to improve the welfare of the entire nation? Should all persons within a society, not just those who can afford them or have the power to obtain them, have access to family planning programs and contraceptives?

Of course all nations do not answer these questions in the same way, nor do different cultural, age, and gender groups within a country agree on responses. Consider China, a country of more than a billion people with an increase of 15 million each year. The government has established a policy that limits couples to one child. Couples must pay a fine if they exceed the limit. Such a policy offends people who believe that choices in procreation should be left to individuals and families. But Xu Tian-Min, vice president of China's Beijing Medical University, argues:

> *Unlimited population expansion threatens to produce disastrous results and eventually jeopardize individuals' personal benefit and value. Therefore, effective birth control and family planning are essential.... The government supports married couples' voluntary use of a number of contraceptive means, including sterilization and elective abortion. Birth control services are provided by various regional health care institutions. This policy is grounded in public welfare arguments.*[6]

Yet China's policy is controversial within as well as outside the country. Traditionally, Chinese families have believed that large numbers of children, particularly boys, bring good fortune. In rural areas, boys help with the farm work and care for elderly family members. The worst thing to befall a family is to be childless or to have only girls.

Even though Chinese women now work in many kinds of jobs and own property (once forbidden), many rural families still believe that girls are a burden until they get married and become someone else's responsibility. If a girl is born, "families routinely lie, cheat or pay fines in order to try a second pregnancy in the hope of having a son," according to a report in

Time magazine. "And female infanticide—plus its modern variation, the misuse of amniocentesis to identify female fetuses in order to abort them—continues. The problem is so extensive that government campaigns urge parents to 'Love your daughter' and allow girl babies to live."[7]

People in other Asian countries have also practiced female infanticide. Parents may starve baby girls, feed them poisonous berries, or smother them. Because of the long-standing preference for male children, men in the thirty to forty-five age group outnumber women by more than ten to one, and some governments have restricted the use of amniocentesis to determine the sex of a fetus.[8]

Amniocentesis for sex selection is officially banned in India, but the practice continues and is even encouraged by some doctors, according to Indian journalist Vimal Balasubrahmanyan. She charges that the nation's family planning policies, which have been in effect since the 1950s, have concentrated so heavily on controlling population that the health needs of women have been overshadowed. Government programs offer women cash incentives to be sterilized (through hysterectomies) or to use contraceptives, usually the Pill or implants. Abortions are also legal and acceptable. But the programs for the most part do not provide basic health care or follow-up programs to treat possible complications or side-effects of using birth control devices. Nor do they emphasize contraceptive use by men or that men as well as women should take responsibility for family planning.[9]

Quite different policies are in effect in Poland. Since Poland, with the help of the Catholic Church, gained its freedom from communist rule in 1989, the Church has been pressing for legislation that would promote its social agenda. Lawmakers passed stricter divorce laws and established religion classes in public schools. Some legislators have pressed for bans on contraceptives and abortion.

Early in 1991, the Polish government, which subsidizes health care, passed regulations that raised the price of contraceptives. Just a year before, Parliament restricted legal abortions by requiring women to obtain the approval of two gynecologists and a psychologist before the procedure could be performed in state hospitals.

The contraceptive and abortion issues, however, have created passionate debates. Most Polish women work outside the home and want to limit the number of children they have. But the government, under pressure from the Catholic Church, introduced an anti-abortion bill that would criminalize abortion and outlaw the sale of contraceptives. Even though 95 percent of the Polish people consider themselves Catholic, a majority has supported a 1956 law that legalizes abortion during the first twelve weeks of a pregnancy.

An estimated 600,000 abortions are performed in Poland annually, according to government statistics, but many people believe the actual number is closer to 1 million. Although Parliament voted against repealing the 1956 law legalizing abortion, women's groups in Poland believe that the Church, with the support of President Lech Walesa, will continue to exert pressure for its policies on reproductive matters. Some feminists believe that women may be forced to become childbearing machines, and may lose many of their rights and freedoms. As one woman said, "We have traded a red regime for one that wears black robes."[10]

WHO'S IN CHARGE?

Wherever governments attempt to establish reproductive policies, whether to prevent or promote childbearing, the issue of women's control over their bodies has taken on ever more importance.

Of course, women living under tyrannical governments are not likely to have many choices about *any* aspects of their lives. And this can mean forced pregnancy, compulsory medical intervention, and certain required behaviors during pregnancy and childbirth. In a democratic society, such coercion is not only repugnant but unjust to women. To paraphrase a rabbi of the seventeenth century, women should not be required to procreate and populate the world by enslaving and destroying themselves.

The wisest approach on reproductive matters in democratic countries seems to be encouraging public debate and allowing people from all walks of life to make informed decisions about their personal lives. People then should be able to act freely upon those decisions—unless the actions infringe upon the rights of others. Common sense and the principles of personal freedom and justice suggest that in matters of reproduction, women should have access to the knowledge and the means to make their own decisions about childbearing.

SOURCE NOTES

Chapter One

1. Jean Seligmann with Donna Foote, "Whose Baby Is It, Anyway?" *Newsweek*, October 28, 1991, p. 73.

2. Michele Cook, "Sobering Dilemma," *St. Paul Pioneer Press Dispatch*, March 1, 1992.

3. Anne C. Roark, "Couple Back Home with Their Embryo," *Los Angeles Times*, September 26, 1989.

Chapter Two

1. Ruth Hubbard, *The Politics of Women's Biology* (New Brunswick, NJ: Rutgers University Press, 1990), pp. 162–163.

2. June Stephenson, *Women's Roots* (Napa, CA: Diemer, Smith Publishing Company, 1988), pp. 41–52.

3. Susan Faludi, *Backlash: The Undeclared War Against American Women* (New York: Crown Publishers, 1991), p. 414.

4. Margaret L. Usdansky, "Baby Boomers Hit Brakes After Life in the Fast Lane," *USA Today*, June 24, 1993.

Chapter Three

1. Marian Segal, "Norplant Birth Control at Arm's Reach," *FDA Consumer*, May 1991, pp. 9–11.

2. Associated Press, "Promising Outlook for a Male 'Pill'," *Chicago Tribune*, June 23, 1991.

3. Suzanne Wymelenberg for the Institute of Medicine, *Science and Babies: Private Decisions, Public Dilemmas* (Washington, D.C.: National Academy Press, 1990), pp. 62–63.

4. Linda M. Harrington, "Poll Shows Minorities Avoid Birth Control," *Chicago Tribune*, September 22, 1991.

5. Knight-Ridder News, "Broader Sex Education Is Proposed," *Chicago Tribune*, October 17, 1991.

6. Hot Topics Column, "Should Schools Provide Birth Control Devices?" *Los Angeles Times*, August 29, 1991.

7. Associated Press, "Program Cuts Teen Pregnancies," *Chicago Tribune*, October 9, 1991.

8. "Poverty and Norplant," *Philadelphia Inquirer*, December 12, 1990.

9. Vanessa Williams, "Letters to the Editor," *Philadelphia Inquirer*, December 19, 1990.

10. Quoted in Ellen Goodman, "Those Who Would Use Norplant As A Method to Control Women," *Philadelphia Inquirer*, February 19, 1991.

11. Interview on "60 Minutes," November 11, 1991.

12. Helen R. Neuborne, "In the Norplant Case, Good Intentions Make Bad Law," *Los Angeles Times*, March 3, 1991.

13. Adele Clarke, "From Blatant to Subtle Sterilization Abuse" in Rita Arditti, Renate Duelli Klein, and Shelley Minden, eds., *Test-Tube Women* (London and Boston: Pandora Press, 1989 edition), pp. 199–203.

14. George Skelton, Daniel M. Weintraub, and Staff Writers, "Most Support Norplant for Teens, Drug Addicts," *Los Angeles Times*, May 27, 1991.

Chapter Four

1. Roper Center for Public Opinion Research, Gallup Poll, September 5–8, 1991; CBS-*New York Times* poll, June 17–20, 1992; NBC News/*Wall Street Journal* survey, April 17–20, 1993; *Los Angeles Times* survey, June 12–14, 1993.

2. Patricia Jaworski, producer, "Thinking about *The Silent Scream*," an audio documentary, transcribed and published in

Abortion Rights and Fetal 'Personhood', Edd Doerr and James W. Prescott, eds., *Abortion Rights and Fetal 'Personhood'* (Long Beach, CA: Centerline Press. 1990), pp. 55–63.

3. Marjorie Reiley Maguire, "Symbiosis, Biology, and Personalization," paper presented at a Washington, D.C. conference, May 30, 1987, reprinted in Americans for Religious Liberty, *Abortion Rights and Fetal 'Personhood'*, pp. 5–14.

4. *Roe et al. v. Wade, District Attorney of Dallas County,* Supreme Court opinion reprinted in *Abortion Rights and Fetal 'Personhood,'* Appendix A, pp. 116–129. Also: Maureen Harrison and Steve Gilbert, eds. *Landmark Decisions of the United States Supreme Court* (Beverly Hills, CA: Excellent Books, 1991), pp. 91–125.

5. Quoted in Sue Anne Pressley, "Random Crime, or Part of Violent Pattern?" *The Washington Post*, August 24, 1993. Also: Jeffrey Yorke, "On the Dial—For Mark Davis, a Hot Potato," *The Washington Post*, August 17, 1993.

6. Quoted in Al Kamen, "Supreme Court Restricts Right to Abortion," *The Washington Post*, July 4, 1989.

Chapter Five

1. Quoted in Tamar Lewin, "Abortion Rules Force Clinics to Weigh Money and Mission," *The New York Times*, June 26, 1991.

2. Polly Hay, "Abortion Gag Bad Medicine," *The Elkhart Truth*, November 19, 1991.

3. Excerpts from the transcript "Planned Parenthood of Southeastern Pennsylvania v. Casey," *The Washington Post*, June 30, 1992.

4. Quoted in Nell Bernstein, "Self-help Abortion Movement," Pacific News Service, September 13, 1991.

5. Lawrence Lader, *RU-486: The Pill That Could End the Abortion Wars and Why American Women Don't Have It* (Reading, MA: Addison-Wesley, 1991), pp. 24 and 79–83.

6. Quoted in Karen Wright, "Hard to Swallow," *Discover*, January 1991, pp. 86–87.

7. Quoted in Janine DeFao, "$10-Million Gift to Aid in

Push for Availability of Abortion Pill," *Los Angeles Times*, October 3, 1991.

8. David G. Savage, "Supreme Court Blocks Abortion Pill's Return," *Los Angeles Times*, July 18, 1992. Also: Associated Press, "U.S. Criticizes Abortion Pill Court Case," *Los Angeles Times*, July 17, 1992.

Chapter Six

1. Vital Statistics, *The Washington Post*, January 21, 1992.

2. Philip Elmer-Dewitt, "Making Babies," *Time*, September 30, 1991, pp. 56–63.

3. "Beating the Clock," *First for Women*, December 2, 1991, p. 11.

4. Quoted in Gina Kolata, "Young Women Offer to Sell Their Eggs to Infertile Couples," *The New York Times*, November 10, 1991.

5. Suzanne Wymelenberg for the Institute of Medicine, *Science and Babies* (Washington, D.C.: National Academy Press, 1990), p. 140.

6. Paul Lauritzen, "What Price Parenthood?" *Hastings Center Report*, March/April 1990, p. 43. Also: Patricia Spallone, *Beyond Conception* (Granby, MA: Bergin & Garvey Publishers, 1989), pp. 112–132.

7. Gina Kolata, "When Grandmother Is the Mother, Until Birth," *The New York Times*, August 5, 1991.

8. Robyn Rowland, "Decoding Reprospeak," *Ms.*, May/June 1991, pp. 38–41. Also: Katha Pollit, "When Is a Mother Not a Mother?" *The Nation*, December 31, 1990, p. 841.

Chapter Seven

1. From the court opinion reprinted in "Capital Court's Ruling on Fetal Status," *The New York Times*, April 27, 1991.

2. New York Times News Service, "Hospital Makes Policy on Pregnancy Rights," *Chicago Tribune*, November 29, 1990.

3. Anne Detweiler, "Furor Over Fetal Therapy," *Technology Review*, July 1991, p. 17.

4. Quoted in Ruth Hubbard, *The Politics of Women's*

Biology (New Brunswick, NJ: Rutgers University Press, 1990), p. 173. Also: Katha Pollit, "A New Assault on Feminism," *The Nation*, March 26, 1990, p. 415.

5. Lawrence J. Nelson, Ph.D., J.D, and Nancy Milliken, M.D., "Compelled Medical Treatment of Pregnant Women," *Journal of the American Medical Association*, February 19, 1988, p. 1061.

6. Hubbard, p. 175.

7. Earl Ubell, "Are Births As Safe As They Could Be?," *Parade Magazine*, February 7, 1993, pp. 9–11.

8. Hubbard, p. 149.

9. Ann Piccininni, "Nurse/Midwife Builds Confidence With Choices," *Chicago Tribune*, May 5, 1991.

10. Sidney M. Wolfe, M.D., with Rhoda Donkin Jones, *Women's Health Alert* (Reading, MA and Menlo Park, CA: Addison-Wesley, 1991), pp. 73–111.

11. Susan Okie, "Profit Motive Called a Factor in 'Repeat' Cesarean Sections," *The Washington Post*, January 2, 1991.

Chapter Eight

1. Quoted in Robb London, "2 Dismissed in Warning on Alcohol and Pregnancy," *The New York Times*, March 30, 1991.

2. Katha Pollitt, "'Fetal Rights': A New Assault on Feminism," *The Nation*, March 26, 1990, p. 418.

3. Josephine Gittler and Dr. Merle McPherson, "Prenatal Substance Abuse," *Children Today*, July/August 1990, p. 18. Also: Mary Grabar, "Pregnancy Police," *The Progressive*, December 1990, p. 22.

4. Gittler and McPherson, pp. 3–5.

5. Jan Hoffman, "Pregnant, Addicted—And Guilty?" *The New York Times Magazine*, August 19, 1990, pp. 34–35. Also: Pamela Warrick, "The Pregnancy Police," *Los Angeles Times*, October 30, 1991.

6. Barbara Kantrowitz with Vicki Quade, Binnie Fisher, James Hill, and Lucille Beachy, "The Pregnancy Police," *Newsweek*, April 29, 1991, pp. 52–53. Also: "Judge Clears Mother of Passing Cocaine to Infant Daughter," *The New York Times*,

February 5, 1991.

7. Gina Kolata, "Racial Bias Seen on Pregnant Addicts," *The New York Times*, July 20, 1990.

8. James E. Long, "Don't Give Up on Pregnant Addicts," *Chicago Tribune*, September 14, 1991.

9. Children's Defense Fund, "Infant Mortality Rates" (chart), *CDF Reports*, March 1991, p. 4.

10. Devra Lee Davis, "Fathers and Fetuses," *The New York Times*, March 1, 1991. Also: Andrew Purvis, "The Sins of the Fathers," *Time*, November 26, 1990, pp. 90–92. Also: Dan Charles, David Dickson, Roger Lewin, and Stephanie Pain, "Why Men Should Also Think of the Baby," *New Scientist*, March 2, 1991, p. 16.

Chapter Nine

1. Quoted in Gail Schmoller, "Pregnancy, Gender Issues Pose Questions of Ethics," *Chicago Tribune*, September 15, 1991.

2. "New Mexico Supreme Court Affirms $50,000 Award for Pregnancy Bias," *BNA Labor Daily*, January 25, 1991.

3. "Excerpts from Court Ruling on 'Fetal Protection' Policy in Job Screening," *The New York Times*, March 21, 1991.

4. Anne Merewood, "Father Figures," *Chicago Tribune*, September 29, 1991.

Chapter Ten

1. Joseph A. McFalls, Jr., "Population: A Lively Introduction," *Population Bulletin*, October 1991, p. 32.

2. Statistics from Zero Population Growth, Washington, D.C.

3. Martin Howell, "Population Explosion Threatens Future of Beleaguered Pakistan," *Los Angeles Times*, March 17, 1991.

4. Ken Silverstein, "Sterilization Rate Stirs Controversy," *Los Angeles Times*, September 22, 1991.

5. Ruth Macklin, "Ethics and Human Reproduction: International Perspectives," *Social Problems*, February 1990, p. 45.

6. Xu Tian-Min, "China: Moral Puzzles," *Hasting Center Report*, March/April 1990, p. 24.

7. Sandra Burton, "Condolences, It's a Girl," *Time*, Special Issue, Fall 1990, p. 36.

8. "Asia: Discarding Daughters," *Time*, Special Issue, Fall 1990, p. 40.

9. Vimal Balasubrahmanyan, "Women as Targets in India's Family Planning Policy," in *Test-Tube Women* (London and Boston: Pandora Press, 1989), pp. 153–163.

10. Quoted in "Poland Ends Subsidies for the Pill," *Chicago Tribune*, May 10, 1991. Also: Stephen Engelberg, "Anti-Abortion Bill in Poland Dividing Church and Public," *The New York Times*, May 16, 1991. Also: Alan Guttmacher Institute, "Poles Pick Choice Over Church," *Washington Memo No. 8*, May 20, 1991.

GLOSSARY

Abortifacient—a drug or chemical that can cause an abortion.

Antibody—a protein produced by the body to counteract a foreign substance in the body.

Artificial insemination—a procedure to impregnate without sexual intercourse, in which semen is deposited directly in the vagina or uterus.

Cauterize—to apply heat or chemicals to destroy tissue.

Cesarean section—a surgical procedure to extract a fetus.

Cervix—the neck or outer end of the uterus.

Conception—a sperm cell and a ripened egg cell, or ovum, unite to form a fertilized ovum; pregnancy begins.

Condom—a rubber sheath that can be rolled down over the penis before sex to keep sperm out of the vagina and protect against infection.

Contraceptive—any drug, device, or sex technique used to prevent conception.

Diaphragm—a dome-shaped rubber device that fits into the vagina and covers the cervix to prevent sperm from entering the uterus during sex.

Douching—rinsing out the vagina with water, diluted vinegar solution, or other solutions.

Ectopic—"in the wrong place." An ectopic pregnancy is a

dangerous, abnormal condition in which a pregnancy develops in a fallopean tube or in the abdominal cavity instead of inside the uterus.

Elective abortion—an abortion performed at the wish or choice of the woman.

Embryo—the earliest stage of pregnancy from conception to the end of the eighth week in the uterus.

Fallopian Tube—a duct that connects the female ovary area to the uterus, or womb.

Gametes—special sex cells that contain only half the hereditary materials as other cells in the body. The sperm cell is the male gamete. The egg cell or ovum is the female gamete.

Hormone—a chemical originating in the glands and conveyed to all parts of the body.

Hysterectomy—the surgical removal of the uterus.

Infertility—the inability to reproduce.

Laparoscopy—a surgical procedure; a lighted tube is inserted into the abdomen through a tiny incision so that the surgeon can view the ovaries, tubes, and uterus.

In vitro fertilization—an artificial means of conception in which ovum and sperm are combined in a petri dish.

Menopause—the period at which menstruation stops.

Ovulation—the release from the ovary of a ripened egg cell, or ovum; it travels down the fallopian tube toward the uterus.

Ovum (pl. *ova*)—a female reproductive cell, the egg cell.

Placenta—developing inside the uterus during pregnancy, it provides nutrients and oxygen to the growing fetus.

Semen—secretion from the penis that contains sperm.   .

Sperm—male fertilizing cell.

Spermicide—a chemical that kills sperm on contact.

Sterilization—an operation to make a man or woman sterile, unable to reproduce.

Tubal ligation—an operation in which a woman's fallopian tubes are tied and cut on both sides to cause sterilization.

Vasectomy—an operation in which male ducts transporting semen are cut and tied to cause sterilization.

BIBLIOGRAPHY

Books

Annas, George J., and the American Civil Liberties Union. *The Basic ACLU Guide to Patient Rights.* Carbondale and Edwardsville, IL: Southern Illinois University Press, 1989.

Arditti, Rita, and Renate Duelli Klein and Shelley Minden, eds. *Test-Tube Women: What Future for Motherhood?* London and Boston: Pandora Press, 1984.

Corea, Gena. *The Hidden Malpractice: How American Medicine Mistreats Women.* New York: Harper & Row, 1985.

Cozic, Charles, and Stacey Tipp, eds. *Abortion: Opposing Viewpoints.* San Diego, CA: Greenhaven Press, 1991.

Dudley, William, ed. *Genetic Engineering: Opposing Viewpoints.* San Diego, CA: Greenhaven Press, 1990.

Harrison, Beverly Wildung. *Our Right to Choose.* Boston: Beacon Press, 1970.

Hubbard, Ruth. *The Politics of Women's Biology.* New Brunswick, NJ and London: Rutgers University Press, 1990.

Kuklin, Susan. *What Do I Do Now? Talking About Teenage Pregnancy.* New York: G. P. Putnam's Sons, 1991.

Lader, Lawrence. *RU-486: The Pill That Could End the Abortion Wars and Why American Women Don't Have It.* Reading, MA and New York: Addison-Wesley Publishing Company, 1991.

Landau, Elaine. *Surrogate Mothers*. New York: Franklin Watts, 1988.

Leidholdt, Dorchen, and Janice G. Raymond. *The Sexual Liberals and the Attack on Feminism*. New York and Oxford: Pergamon Press, 1990.

McLean, Sheila, and Noreen Burrows. *The Legal Relevance of Gender*. Atlantic Highlands, NJ: Humanities Press International, 1988.

Nourse, Alan E., M.D. *Birth Control*. New York: Franklin Watts, 1988.

Spallone, Patricia. *Beyond Conception: The New Politics of Reproduction*. Granby, MA: Bergin & Garvey Publishers, 1989.

Terkel, Susan Neiburg. *Abortion*. New York: Franklin Watts, 1988.

Women's Research and Education Institute, The. *The American Woman 1990–1991*. New York and London: W.W. Norton and Company, 1990.

Wymelenberg, Suzanne, Institute of Medicine. *Science and Babies*. Washington, D.C.: National Academy Press, 1990.

Articles

Beardsley, Tim. "Aborted Research." *Scientific American*, February 1990, p. 16.

"Beating the Clock." *First for Women*, December 2, 1991, pp. 6–13.

Blakeslee, Sandra. "Fetal Cell Transplants Show Early Promise in Parkinson Patients." *The New York Times*, November 12, 1991.

Budiansky, Stephen, with Kathleen McAuliffe and Erica E. Goode. "The New Rules of Reproduction." *U.S. News & World Report*, April 18, 1988, pp. 66–69.

Byrne, Harry J. "A House Divided: The Pro-Life Movement." *America*, January 12, 1991, pp. 6–10.

"Capital Court's Ruling on Fetal Status." *The New York Times*, April 27, 1990.

Daubenmier, Judy. "Abortion-Rights Activists Heartened by Court Ruling." *South Bend Tribune*, February 21, 1991.

Davis, Devra Lee. "Fathers and Fetuses." *The New York Times*, March 1, 1991.

DeBettencourt, Kathleen B. "The Wisdom of Solomon: Cutting the Cord that Harms." *Children Today*, July–August 1990, pp. 17–20.

Detweiler, Anne. "Furor Over Fetal Therapy." *Technology Review*, July 1991, pp. 16–17.

Elkind, David. "Teens' Privacy Versus Parents' Rights." *Parents*, November 1990, p. 236.

Elmer-Dewitt, Philip. "Making Babies." *Time*, September 30, 1991, pp. 56–63.

Gittler, Josephine and Dr. Merle McPherson. "Prenatal Substance Abuse." *Children Today*, July–August 1990, pp. 3–7.

Goldsmith, Stephen. "Prosecution to Enhance Treatment." *Children Today*, July–August 1990, pp. 13–16.

Grabar, Mary. "Pregnancy Police." *The Progressive*, December 1990, pp. 22–24.

Greenhouse, Linda. "Court Backs Right of Women to Jobs with Health Risks." *The New York Times*, March 21, 1991.

Heaney, Robert P. "RU-486 and Abortion Strategies." *America*, January 12, 1991, pp. 12–13.

Hilts, Philip J. "Anguish Over Medical First: Tissue From Fetus to Fetus." *The New York Times*, April 16, 1991.

Hoffman, Jan. "Pregnant, Addicted—and Guilty?" *The New York Times Magazine*, August 19, 1990, pp. 33–35, 44.

Horowitz, Robert. "A Coordinated Public Health and Child Welfare Response to Prenatal Substance Abuse." *Children Today*, July–August 1990, pp. 8–12.

Hunter, Eva. "For Want of a Child." *The Sunday Oregonian*, October 20, 1991.

"Judge Clears Mother of Passing Cocaine to Infant Daughter." *The New York Times*, February 5, 1991.

Kaimner, Wendy. "The Fetal-Protection Charade." *The New York Times*, April 29, 1990.

Kinsley, Michael. "Life Terms." *The New Republic*, July 15 and 22, 1991, p. 4.

Kirp, David L. "The Pitfalls of 'Fetal Protection.'" *Society*, March–April 1991, pp. 70–76.

Kolata, Gina. "More Babies Being Born to be Donors of Tissue." *The New York Times*, June 4, 1991.

———. "Racial Bias Seen on Pregnant Addicts." *The New York Times*, July 20, 1990.

———. "Young Women Offer to Sell Their Eggs to Infertile Couples." *The New York Times*, November 10, 1991.

Lait, Matt. "Experts Are Critical of Joint Custody Rule by Judge." *Los Angeles Times*, September 28, 1991.

Lewin, Tamar. "Abortion Rules Force Clinics to Weigh Money and Mission." *The New York Times*, June 26, 1991.

London, Robb. "2 Dismissed in Warning on Alcohol and Pregnancy." *The New York Times*, March 30, 1991.

Martin, Alex. "Mom's Blood Refusal Backed." *Newsday*, January 19, 1990, p. 7.

McWilliams, Rita. "Why Aren't Pro-lifers and Pro-choicers Pro-contraception?" *The Washington Monthly*, July/August 1991, pp. 10–18.

Morganthau, Tom. "Target: Wichita." *Newsweek*, August 19, 1991, pp. 18–20.

Morrow, Lance. "When One Body Can Save Another." *Time*, June 17, 1991, pp. 54–58.

Mosher, William D. "Contraceptive Practice in the United States, 1982–1988." *Family Planning Perspectives*, September–October, 1990, pp. 198–214.

Neuhaus, Richard John. "Renting Women, Buying Babies and Class Struggles." *Society*, March–April 1988, pp. 8–22.

Phillips, Leslie. "Consent Laws: Second Front in Abortion Fight." *USA TODAY*, September 10, 1991.

Pollitt, Katha. "A New Assault on Feminism." *The Nation*, March 26, 1990, pp. 409–418.

———. "When Is a Mother Not a Mother?" *The Nation*, December 31, 1990, pp. 828–845.

Post, Stephen G. "Fetal Tissue Transplant: The Right to Question Progress." *America*, January 12, 1991, pp. 14–16.

Purvis, Andrew. "The Sins of the Fathers." *Time*, November 26, 1990, pp. 90–92.

Raymond, Janice G. "International Traffic in Reproduction." *Ms.* May/June 1991, pp. 29–33.

Rosenberg, Tina. "Winning the Trojan War." *The Washington Monthly*, July/August 1991, pp. 18–21.

Rowland, Robyn. "Decoding Reprospeak." *Ms.* May/June 1991, pp. 38–41.

Segal, Marian. "Norplant Birth Control at Arm's Reach." *FDA Consumer*, May 1991, pp. 9–11.

Seligmann, Jean, with Donna Foote. "Whose Baby Is It, Anyway?" *Newsweek*, October 28, 1991, p. 73.

Simon, Howard A. "Fetal Protection Policies after Johnson Controls: No Easy Answers." *Law Journal*, Spring 1990, pp. 491–511.

Simons, Andrew. "Brave New Harvest." *Christianity Today*, November 19, 1990, pp. 24–28.

Stellman, Jeanne Mager, and Joan E. Bertin. "Science's Anti-Female Bias." *The New York Times*, June 4, 1990.

"The Future of Abortion." *Newsweek*, July 17, 1989, pp. 14–27.

Wattleton, Faye. "Reproductive Rights Are Fundamental Rights." *The Humanist*, January–February 1991, pp. 21 and 42–43.

"Why Men Should Also Think of the Baby." *New Scientist*, March 2, 1991, p. 16.

Wilkerson, Isabel. "Michigan Judges Berated on Abortion Comments." *The New York Times*, May 3, 1991.

Williams, Patricia J. "Reflections on Law, Contracts, and the Value of Life." *Ms.* May/June 1991, pp. 42–46.

Woodward, Kenneth L. "Equal Rights, Equal Risks." *Newsweek*, April 1, 1991, pp. 56 and 59.

Wright, Karen. "Hard to Swallow." *Discover*, January 1991, pp. 86–87.

Zelizer, Viviana A. "From Baby Farms to Baby M." *Society*, March–April 1988, pp. 23–28.

Zielinski, Christine. "The Toxic Trap." *Personnel Journal*, February 1990, pp. 40–49.

INDEX

forms of, 17–19, 88, 89, 90, 91
information about, 20, 88
laws affecting, 20, 92, 93
myths regarding, 21
religious beliefs about, 16–17, 89, 90, 92, 93
and privacy issues, 20
and welfare mothers, 24–25
Birth defects, 70, 79
Birth rate, 87
Bremmer, Lynn, 73, 74
Bush, George, 39, 43, 45, 46

Calder, Angela, 61–63
Center for Reproductive Law and Policy, 45
Cesarean section, 62, 67, 68, 89, 90
Childbirth, 7, 61–85
Children's Defense Fund (CDF), 23, 77
Clinton, Bill, 18, 39
Community and Migrant Health Center, 77
Condoms, 17
Cryopreservation, 52. See also Embryos, frozen

Diabetes, 46
Drug abuse, 5, 6, 8, 27, 71–76

Ectrodactylism, 5
Egg donor programs, 53–54
Embryos, 6, 17, 18, 28, 51, 53, 55, 56

frozen, 52–53
implanted, 6, 50–53, 58

Family planning programs, 16, 19, 88, 89, 91
Female infanticide, 91, 92
Feminist Majority Foundation (FMF), 44
Fetal alcohol syndrome, 70
Fetal personhood, 29–31
"Fetal protection" policies, 82–85
Fetal therapy, 8, 64
Fetal tissue transplants, 45–47
Fetus, 7, 30, 55, 60, 61, 62, 63, 64, 65, 68, 69, 80, 82, 83, 92
and alcohol, 70, 72
and drugs, 71–76, 78
Food and Drug Administration (FDA), 18, 43, 44, 45
Freedom of Choice Act, 42

"Gag rule, the," 38–39
Gamete intra-fallopian transfer (GIFT), 51
Gender roles, 13
Genetics, 54–56
Genetic disorders, 55

Health and Human Services Administration, 46
Human immunodeficiency virus (HIV), 22, 72
Hysterectomies, 18, 92